Much Ado
About
TEXAS

Norma

Eaton

Publishing Coordinator – Sharon Kizziah-Holmes

Paperback-Press
an imprint of A & S Publishing
A & S Holmes, Inc.

ISBN -13: 978-1-951772-09-3

Acknowledgments

To my husband, Gary, for sharing the love we have. Love for each other, love for our family, love of music, and love of God, who surely smiled when He brought us together. Thank you for a great life.

CHAPTER ONE

Cassidy Palmer glanced briefly at her father's irate expression and continued tossing clothes into her suitcase.

"You what?" He waved an envelope in the air. "You're resigning?" She was sure the entire population of Boston could hear John Palmer's ranting. "I just learned about your leaving," he bellowed. "You never said a thing. Why didn't you tell me earlier?" He didn't wait for an answer. "I could have stopped this nonsense. I've been talking to Kyle." He walked toward her. "You remember Kyle, the fiancé you dumped without giving me a clue. He seems to think you two could work things out. After all, it's been several weeks since the breakup. Don't you think you've carried this silent treatment you're giving him long enough?"

"I don't want to talk about it."

"Well, I want to. Kyle is a big asset to our

company. He's brought a number of new clients in. The two of you would be..." His breath came out in a snort. "I don't even know why you broke up with him."

"I fell in love, he didn't. It's that simple." She wadded a nightgown into a ball and stuffed it into her bag.

"That's not true, Cass. He is crazy about you."

"Crazy, but not about me."

"He's perfect for you!" He slapped the envelope he was holding against the wall in a tirade.

"On paper."

"What's that supposed to mean?"

She finally turned and faced him. "You introduced me to *your* perfect man because his attributes were extremely suitable for Palmer Corporation, and, oh yes, he was smart, charming and attentive and I fell hard." Tears welled in her eyes.

"Then what's the problem? There must be some logical explanation for this."

"Oh, there is. Her name is Charlotte."

John Palmer's mouth dropped open. "Another woman?" He rolled his eyes toward the ceiling. "I can't believe he would cheat on you."

She smiled as she closed her last suitcase. "Oh, I think it is the other way around. I cheated on the other woman. I didn't want to tell you this because you think the sun rises and sets in him." She took a long breath. "I'm sorry, Father, for not telling you, and you do deserve an explanation." Tears stung her eyes as she took a shuddering breath. "He's been married to Charlotte all along. My best friend,

Sheila, saw him while having dinner in a restaurant with her mother in a little town about forty miles from here. Sheila's mother lives there and knew the 'happy couple'. She told Sheila she'd went to their wedding a few years ago."

Fury clearly sounded in his voice. "If this is true, I'll take care of him."

"Don't, Father. I think his wife has enough on her plate just being married to that money-hungry, philandering cuss. Besides, I'm leaving. I don't ever want to see or hear about that jerk again. I should have suspected something long before I found out. All those out of town business meetings on the weekends."

He glanced at her packed bags. "Where are you going?"

"Texas. The taxi should be here any minute to take me to the airport."

John Palmer paced back and forth for a few seconds and whirled toward her. "Texas! You've lived in Boston your entire life. What will you do in Texas?"

"Stay on a farm."

"Is this some kind of a joke?"

"No joke, Father. Sheila told me about her and her brother Brad's friend who lives in Texas. They told him about me and asked if I could come stay on his farm for a while. He was very receptive and said I could stay in a cabin behind the main house. I corresponded with him online and he seemed really nice. He sent his picture to me so he wouldn't seem like a stranger when we met." She looked her father in the eye. "I prayed a lot about this and I'm going.

He's invited me to stay in his guest house as long as I want."

"You prayed! Ha! What's prayer got to do with anything?"

It always broke her heart that her father did not believe in prayer. When her mother was alive, they prayed often together. She missed those times. Her daily prayer is that her father would become a believer.

He let his breath out noisily. "This is crazier than I thought. You are not going to Texas to meet a stranger you met online. I'll not have it! You do remember you're a junior partner and we have stockholders to think about. I'll have to renounce you as a partner and you won't get a dime from the company. What will people think? This ridiculous humiliation could ruin the business."

"The business. Yes, that's the important thing here. Not that a creep broke your daughter's heart and strongly 'suggested' she use her trust fund to invest in a 'great deal he had in mind'. Well, don't worry. I don't need your money. I'll be just fine. Fortunately, I still have the savings Mother left me." Catching her breath, she continued. "Besides, it's not how it looks. I did not just meet a man online. He's Sheila's and Brad's best friend they've known since childhood."

"You're not thinking with a clear mind. You're willing to give up your life here, your position with the company to live on a farm? What will you do on a farm? Your idea of roughing it is when your favorite table is not available at the country club."

She glared at him. "I believe you're describing

Kyle, not me." She let her breath out. "I am going to Texas and stay on Sheila's friend's farm and that's that. I don't have to know anything about farming. I plan to rest, relax, and enjoy the quiet beauty of the wide-open spaces. Can't you understand I need a change of atmosphere?" She tried to take his hand but he pulled away. "You know I never wanted to join the firm. I did it to please you. My desire was to use my teaching degree."

Her father interrupted. "And make one-tenth of the salary you're making now? You have lost your mind."

"I'm leaving, Father. I haven't been a proper employee for you since this all took place with Kyle. I'm sure you can find a suitable replacement for me."

"Well don't bother to come crawling back. It's going to be hard enough explaining your absence...I'll have to make up a feasible excuse for the stockholders." His frown gave her chills.

She walked by him pulling two bags on rollers behind her. "Goodbye, Father. Have a great life. I wish you much success in your 'business'." She bit her tongue for speaking to her father in such a manner, then turned her head toward him. "I love you, and I pray that someday you'll understand why I need to leave Boston."

As the plane landed in Houston, Cass thought to herself. *Forgive me, dear God. Maybe I am crazy?* She shook her head and whispered to herself, "No, I had to get out of Boston. I do not want to see the looks on people's faces Kyle and I met this past year who just knew we were destined for marriage." She thought wistfully for a moment picturing her dream. Marriage, kids and a picket fence... "I guess he'll have all that. Just not with me."

During the long shuttle ride from the airport to Pine Valley, she had time to reflect on what she was doing. Too late now. She definitely could not go back home, not the way her father felt about her. Sheila's brother Brad swore Jake Carpenter was one of the finest men he had ever known, and his farm in Texas was just what she needed to relax and forget about the woes of Boston.

As she stepped out of the shuttle to retrieve her luggage, her throat felt like she had swallowed a wad of cotton. The heat and dust were overwhelming. About as overwhelming as being pinned between a businessman who smelled of cigar smoke and a portly woman who snored. She couldn't wait for a cold drink of water and then a soothing bath. She pulled her handkerchief from her pocket and dabbed at the perspiration that beaded on her forehead.

A strong-armed man reached past her to help with her bags. Noting the man's clothes were as dusty as the air around her, she held her hand over her nose as he slapped his hat against the side of his leg to shake loose some of the powdery grime. Six children who varied in age huddled around him. One hung onto his leg like it was a tree trunk.

Cassidy smiled politely at the sooty family and turned her attention to the building directly in front of her. The crooked shingle hanging from rusted nails read, "H TEL." She sidestepped a lone tumbleweed as it blew past and again patted at the perspiration trickling down her neck. Was Texas always this hot? She held her hand up to shade her eyes from the merciless July sun and tried to quell her dizziness. Perhaps Jake was waiting inside.

"Are you Cassidy Palmer?" came a deep-timbered voice from behind.

She turned. It was the dust-covered man with all the children. "Why, yes, I am."

He nodded. "Thought you might be. I'm Jake Carpenter."

She stared a long embarrassing moment with a dropped jaw. "I...I'm sorry. You look different from the picture you sent on e-mail."

"Well, I was dressed in my Sunday best for that picture. We've been cleaning the cabin getting it ready for your arrival."

His broad smile showed the beautiful white teeth that was in his picture. "Yes, yes," she stammered. "Of course, you're Jake Carpenter and I'm Cassidy Palmer."

"I think we established that already." He chuckled as he picked up her bags. "Are these all you have?"

She nodded as a small girl came over to feel Cass's dress while twin boys took hold of her hands and smiled up with toothless grins. The other siblings made a slow scrutinizing circle around her.

"You — you have six children?" she choked out.

"Actually seven. The baby's asleep in the wagon."

"Wag...on?"

"Well, I didn't know how much baggage you'd have and didn't think it would all fit in my van with all of us, plus the kids love to ride in the back of the wagon, so..."

Her mind whirled as did her gaze toward a horse that had just let out a snort. He was hitched to a wooden wagon with a small toddler peering over the side. Seven kids, a horse and wagon, on a farm... seven kids? So much for quiet relaxation. Dizziness took over as she crumbled to the ground in a dead faint.

"Step back. Give her air," said a woman

"She's coming 'round," said another.

"What happened to her?" a child asked.

"Heat's too much for a city slicker. I understand she comes from up east---Boston, I think," a man scoffed.

Cass clearly heard noises and chattering but could barely distinguish voices. Raising up on her elbows, she managed to open one eye against the blazing sun. Everything was hazy, but she could make out several young faces staring down on her.

"Is she sickly, Pa?" one of the twins asked.

The other asked, "Will you have to have the Vet shoot her? Like he did Bessie?"

"Bessie was a very sick cow, son. You don't shoot sick people."

A sick cow? Cassidy moaned. It all came back to her. Seven children, wagon, farm, horse, sick cows... She fell backwards and covered her face with her hands. She could almost hear her father's scathing voice yelling I told you so.

Jake knelt beside her. "Stand back and let me help Miss Palmer up." Effortlessly, he scooped her into his arms as onlookers parted to let him through to the "H TEL" lobby. He deposited her on a leather settee, and then placed a pillow under her head.

"Dillon," he called to his oldest son, "get Miss Palmer a glass of water."

Cass lifted her eyelids and stared back at the softest most concerned eyes she had ever seen. Blue ⸺ his eyes were definitely blue ⸺ with darker rims that appeared to see through to her very soul. Her pulse quickened at the tenderness his gaze possessed.

She blinked a few times to focus. "You have sick cows?"

Jake sighed. "No. Bessie was extremely sick and dying and the Vet had to put her out of her misery immediately. The twins heard the shot and I explained there was no other way. Sorry if that upset you. My boy is bringing you some water. You are probably dehydrated." He brushed a strand of hair from her face. "By the way, your red hair is lovely."

She smiled a thank you and raised her head slightly, then dropped it back. His hand was callused, but his touch was surprisingly tender, almost a caress. "Water will be nice, Mr. Carpenter, but it's an explanation I really need. Your e-mails didn't say anything about children. I'm sure you have your hands full and don't need another person to deal with. I'll just get a room."

Jake's gaze darted around the room, then back to her. "I assumed Sheila or Brad told you all about me."

She shook her head. "They only told me you were a really nice friend who offered a place for me to visit to get over... never mind. I'll make a reservation here."

"Nonsense. You will stay in the cabin behind the main house." He shifted nervously and continued. "The kids won't be a bother. Besides once you get acquainted, they might grow on you."

She raised to a seated position. "You thought seven children would grow on me?"

"But in our e-mails, you mentioned you loved and wanted children."

She did say that, but obviously not in the way he took it. "I meant if I ever married, I wanted to have children."

"Well, I hope you do someday. Children are God's gift. Treasure them." He stared at his fingernails, then back to her. "Their mother wasn't much older than you when we had Beth, our oldest."

Sadness engulfed her. "Sheila told me you had lost your wife. I'm so sorry."

"Ma's dead, not lost," came the young girl's stern voice. "People said it was God's will. He took her. I hate God!"

Cass turned and saw a dark-haired girl dressed in a gray dress. She held a toddler clad in a diaper. The little tyke looked to be around one or two years old. The older girl's jaw jutted in defiance. It was easy to see she wanted to say a lot more.

Jake interrupted to introduce his daughter. "This is Beth. She's twelve. She's been the woman of the house since…" He stopped short, rose and took the toddler from Beth, then sat down beside Cass. "This is Baby Faye. She turned eighteen months a couple weeks ago." He tweaked the child's nose and made her laugh.

Cass turned her attention to Beth. "Honey, my mother died also. I was older than you, but it was hard. We don't know the reason for a lot of things that happen, but I'm sure God had a good reason for taking our mothers. He probably wanted two more perfect angels."

A frown crossed Beth's forehead. "You don't know that! He took my mom and I will never forgive Him."

Before Cass could say anything further, the toddler reached for the locket that hung around Cass's neck and immediately placed it in her mouth. Cass bent close to Jake to keep the chain from breaking. The smell of dust and her perfume stirred in the air as they leaned into each other.

Beth hurried to pull the locket from Baby Faye's mouth. "No, no," she said very motherly then took the child from her father.

Cass pulled herself away from Jake. "It's okay. All babies like trinkets. She won't hurt it."

Beth turned her back, cuddling Baby Faye close to her chest.

"She's protective," Jake said of Beth. "It hasn't been easy on her."

"When did their mother pass away?"

Jake swallowed hard and nervously turned his hat in his hands. "Right after Faye was born."

Cass softened. "Must be devastating to lose your

wife in childbirth."

"It wasn't childbirth," he muttered.

She waited.

"It wasn't childbirth," he repeated.

She patted his hand. "It isn't any of my business. Sorry."

Jake turned his hat again. That wasn't all Cass noticed. There was that muscle in his jaw that flexed just before he spoke and the softening of his features when he studied her... like now.

His gaze traveled from her hair to her eyes, then lingered a little too long. Clearing his throat, he said, "It's just...there's no reason to discuss it." Then he smiled, "You're our guest and you're here to have a great, restful time void of any unpleasantness." Then he outright chuckled. "That's my exact orders from Sheila and Brad. Let you enjoy your time here and, by the way, you're welcome as long as you want to stay."

"Thank you, Jake, but I still feel I'd be a burden on all of you. I need to make a reservation here at the hotel."

"Stop it. You're not a burden and as much as I love my kids, it might be nice to have an adult conversation once in a while — that is, if you ever feel like talking." He hung his head. "Also, this was once a hotel but it was abandoned for several years and it's now mostly a saloon with a small eatery, so there are no rooms to rent. Sorry. Guess you're stuck with us."

Just then the boy returned with a glass of water, his hair plastered straight across his forehead with an overabundance of hair cream. He wore a blue chambray shirt and jeans. He rubbed his dusty shoes on the back of his trouser legs, then announced politely, "I'm Dillon, Miss Palmer."

"Thank you, Dillon. Call me Cass." She gratefully took the glass from him and smiled at his boyish attempt to make himself presentable. After drinking every last drop, she handed the tumbler back. "You're quite a gentleman, Dillon. How old are you?"

"Ten, Miss...Cass." A hint of bashfulness skimmed his features. "Do you want another?"

"I'm fine. Thank you for asking."

The rest of the children filed in and Cass likened it to a parade as they formed a row in front of her. With the exception of Beth and Dillon, they all were barefooted and their hair was a bit windblown; but their smiles were contagious and Cass found herself smiling back at them.

Dillon placed his hand on top of his little brother's head. "This is Bobby. He's three. He don't talk much 'cause the twins do his talkin' for him, but he's not dumb."

Bobby clung to his father's leg as he had earlier. He shyly peeked around at Cass.

The twins stepped forward and each told her their names. Ronald and Donald. "But you can call us Ronnie and Donnie, everybody does. We're almost six. We're going to go to school this year."

Their exuberance about school clearly showed in their grins that spread from ear to ear. "Nice to meet you boys," she returned.

"Are you going to be our new Ma?" Ronnie asked.

Cass felt her cheeks flush. "Your what?"

Jake stepped forward. "Boys, why would you ask such a question? Behave yourselves."

Dillon interjected, "Bobby's not dumb, but the twins are."

"I'm not dumb," Ronnie said. "She looks like that picture in Pa's book."

"Oh?" A book? Cass didn't know what to expect next.

"Pa's book he orders stuff from," Ronnie explained.

"Ah, a catalog," Cass said relieved.

Donnie interrupted. "Yeah, I know the picture. She's got long curly hair like yours, and she's pointin' at a plow. Pa looks at that picture and gets all funny sounding when he says…" He lowered his voice to mock his father. "Sure would like to have one of those someday."

Heat spread over Cass's cheeks again when she caught a glimpse of Jake, his hat twirling into a blur.

"Okay, boys, that's enough." Then he looked at Cass. "I…I've been needing a new plow." He tried to sound sincere, but he knew his grin gave him away.

Cass glanced back at the twins' innocent faces. She couldn't tell them apart, so she'd already forgotten who was who.

A curly haired blond girl stood with her head hanging down so far Cass had to lean sideways to see the child's face. "And who are you?"

"Tell Cass your name," Jake prodded.

"Ma-Ma-Mary," the girl said meekly. "I-I-I'm

se-se-seven a…and a…ha…half."

The twins giggled and mocked their sister. "Ma-Ma-Mary…"

"Boys," Jake admonished. "That's enough of that." He turned to Cass. "Mary has trouble getting her words out sometimes."

"I used to stutter," Cass revealed before she thought.

Beth took Mary by the arm and pulled her toward the door. "She talks fine. Just don't like strangers!"

"I didn't mean to make her uncomfortable," Cass said to Jake.

"You didn't. It's Beth. Like I said…she's awfully protective."

"That's what I mean, Jake. I need to stay somewhere else. You have a very lovely family, but I don't want to make Beth or any of your children feel ill at ease." She looked out the front entrance. "Is there another hotel in town? One with rooms to rent…with a bath?"

Jake shook his head. "Afraid not. Pine Valley prides itself on staying just the way it was. I know by some people's standards we are extremely behind in amenities found in the city, but we like it here. It's peaceful and everybody loves everybody. There's nothing any of these people wouldn't do to help each other."

"That's very commendable, but…"

"No buts. You'll be very comfortable in the cabin. It does have electricity and running water if that's what you're concerned about."

"That's not it. I just feel I'm imposing."

Jake continued. "We have a grocery store with a pharmacy in the back next to the doctor's office. There's a mercantile that has anything one might need for the home; bedding, curtains, etc. The Vet runs the feed store along with his wife. Also, you'll love the Pine Valley Grace Church on the outskirts of town. We'll go by it on the way home. Might stop in and give our blessings for your safe trip here."

"Jake, it's not Pine Valley, it's not Texas, it's just that I…"

"Oh, and there's Miss Ellie's shop." He chuckled. "She calls it SEW and SEW." He spelled out the SEW. "But don't let the name fool you. People come from as far as Houston and Dallas for her to make their wedding dresses. That lady can sew anything!"

"I'm sure, but you're still not listening."

"Yes, I am and I'm sorry things are not what you expected, but if you just give it a try, I'm sure you will love the farm and it will be a good place to forget…"

She stared at him. "Forget? Did Sheila say something?"

"No, not really. She just said you needed to get away. You had had some unpleasantness that upset you. I didn't ask what and she didn't say what." He shrugged. "None of my business. I just told them you were welcome…and you certainly are. Please don't make me get in all kinds of trouble with Sheila and Brad. Now let's go." He extended his hand to her, then called to his children. "Get in the wagon, kids, we're going home. We'll cook some hotdogs and hamburgers on the grill."

The children all yelled, "Yea!" and ran for the wagon.

Jake took Cass's hand and pulled her along with the rest of the group as Dillon loaded her bags in the wagon.

There was nothing she could do at this point but go along. She couldn't help but look to the heavens and pray to God. The only thing she could think to ask God was to mouth silently, "HELP!"

Beth climbed on the wagon and sat next to where Jake would sit. She was holding tight to Baby Faye.

Jake pointed to her and said politely, "Sweetie, you and Faye need to sit in the back with the rest. Miss Palmer will be sitting up front with me this time."

Beth glared but slowly turned around, handed the baby to Dillon then jumped into the back, plopped down and crossed her arms with a jerk.

CHAPTER TWO

Cass had never ridden on a buckboard and prayed her innards would survive the trip. The wagon was pulled by a horse Jake called Dude. Dude was a champion snorter as he would loudly do every few minutes. When the wagon stopped, the snorting stopped.

Jake turned to her. "Here we are. I hope you don't mind stopping by the church for a few minutes."

"Not at all." She was thankful for the relief.

The small church looked very inviting with stained glass windows and a huge cross as a steeple. When they all entered, Cass felt at peace for the first time since she arrived until she turned around and saw Beth sitting in the back pew, head turned away with a scowl on her face. It was so very sad the child hated God for her mother's death.

Baby Faye was holding her arms out for

someone to take her from her older sister. Cass wanted to but, afraid of upsetting Beth, thought better of it.

"I'll get her," Jake said. "You go on up to the altar with the boys. Please don't let Beth upset you. She'll be fine. She hasn't gone to the altar since her mother passed. I don't want to push it. I'm sure she'll come around one of these days."

Cass whispered, "I hope so. It's so sad to lose your mother. My heart breaks for her." She watched Jake walk back to retrieve the toddler who giggled when her father lifted her in the air. Cass marveled at what a good dad Jake was to his children. It had to be hard raising them all alone, but he seemed to be doing a great job.

Jake joined them at the altar and after they all kneeled, he asked Dillon to say a prayer first.

Dillon smiled and looked up at the picture of Jesus on the front wall. "Dear Lord, thank you for everything we have. Thank you for a safe trip for Miss Pal...Cass." He grinned at Cass and she patted him on the shoulder and mouthed a thank you.

Mary nodded and said, "Sa...same here, Je...Jesus."

"Your turn, twins," Jake said, adding, "whoever wants to go first, go ahead."

They both started talking at once. Ronnie shoved Donnie with his shoulder and Donnie shoved back, talking loudly, "Thank you Jesus for sending us such a pretty visitor."

Ronnie interjected, "Dummy, you're supposed to mention her safe trip."

"Oh, yeah." Donnie looked up to the heavens.

"Lord, she got here okay, got sick later, okay now, I think. Don't have to shoot her. Thanks."

Jake glanced toward Cass and they both stifled a laugh. He shrugged his shoulders and shifted the baby to one arm, taking Cass's hand in his. "Lord, I think everything has been said that needs to be said by the children. We ask your blessings over Miss Palmer and we pray her visit with us gives her the peace she deserves. Amen."

At the word 'Amen', the kids all rose and ran toward the exit.

Cass pulled her hand from Jake's and placed it on his shoulder. "Thanks for stopping here. It is just what I needed. And your boys' prayers were nice, especially about not having to shoot me."

Jake closed his eyes and shook his head. "Sorry about that. They mean well."

Cass smiled. "At least one of them called me pretty. That's a good thing, I guess."

Jake looked at her and winked. "My boy has excellent taste, I'd say."

Cass bit her lip. "Don't you know you're not supposed to flirt in church?"

"Hmmm, where does it say that in the Bible?"

"I'm sure it's in there somewhere. You know, 'Thou shalt not something, something, and something'..."

Jake rose and extended his hand to help her up. "Perhaps we need to get to the farm before I get into more trouble."

"Good idea," she said as they walked out.

Back onboard the wagon, Cass held on for another bumpy ride. "How far away is your farm?"

"Not far. Fifteen minutes or so."

She already felt the bones in her body rearranging again. Trying to make light conversation, she asked, "What do you do on your farm?"

"I raise a lot of crops — hay, corn, beans and cattle. I have probably close to a hundred head of cattle. I buy calves in the spring, raise them until they are full grown, and then sell them."

She smiled at him. "Any sick cows?"

He laughed. "No. All are well. Bessie was our milk cow and she developed a horrendous disease...well, you know the rest. I hated it had to be done. The kids thought of her as a pet."

"They seem to have accepted it well."

"Yeah, they understand. Farm living is sometimes a little hard, but mostly rewarding. I can't imagine living any other way."

Cass couldn't even imagine it at all.

Finally, they pulled in front of a large two-story house nestled between a huge barn and several small sheds. The cabin in question was several feet behind the house. It was small but well maintained, even flowers planted along the sides. She figured she didn't need a lot of room for rest and relaxing.

Jake lifted her down effortlessly. She couldn't help but notice how strong he was as he gently placed her feet on solid ground.

Without warning, a giant yellow Lab came bounding toward her, raised his front legs and placed them on her shoulders and licked her up the side of her face. She let out a frightened moan.

Dillon yelled at the dog. "Down, Buck!"

Fortunately, the dog obeyed and Cass breathed a sigh of relief. One of the twins, she didn't know which, hugged the dog and then looked up at her. "He likes you."

"I…I've never seen a dog so big. I thought it was a pony."

The boy laughed so hard he fell over. "A pony? He just wanted a kiss."

She swiped at her cheek with the back of her hand. "So that's what it was. Don't think I've ever had a dog kiss."

Buck wasn't the only animal greeting her, there was also a calico cat and four kittens. Mixed in among the animals were a flock of geese, several chickens and a tom turkey which Cass learned quickly did not take kindly to strangers. When the turkey came for her, the twins grabbed it and wrestled it to the ground. Bobby laughed so hard he wet his pants. Beth strolled through the chaos carrying the baby and brushed past Cass without a word, grabbed Bobby's hand and scolded him for dirtying his pants and literally dragged him into the house. Jake, apparently oblivious to the commotion, called to Dillon to help unhitch the wagon.

Cass could only stand and stare at the fracas with her mouth open. "So this is rest and relaxation on a Texas farm."

As Cass relaxed on the front porch step still catching her breath, Mary walked up to her and sat down beside her. The child smiled sweetly as she tugged at a strand of Cass's hair.

"You…you're pr…pretty."

Cass pulled Mary onto her lap and held on to her like a life raft in a storm. "Thank you, sweetheart. You'll never know how much I needed a friendly face right now."

She watched Jake and Dillon walk toward the cabin from the barn, carrying her bags between them. Dillon kicked clods of dirt and Jake threw a stick for Buck to fetch. She couldn't help but think what a happy family they were. She prayed Beth could one day soon join in the happiness the others enjoyed, that Beth would be filled with God's grace and mercy.

Jake smiled broadly and waved to Cass. As she waved back, she thought if there were a thousand smiles lined up in a row, his would be the one to win the blue ribbon. Frowning, she gave herself a mental slap. What's wrong with me? It must be the heat getting to me again. Not only did she notice his appealing smile, but also his blond hair streaked by the sun and his muscled physique. She could still feel his strong arms lifting her from the wagon.

She ran her fingers through Mary's curls, the same color of her father's. She imagined how Mary would look with ribbons in her hair and a ruffled pinafore. Cass suddenly brought her mind back to sanity. She didn't need to be thinking about how any of this family would look in anything, and certainly not be admiring the looks of a man with seven kids, a field of cows, a huge dog, horse and sundry other animals. She needed to remind herself why she was here…rest, relaxation and forget…old what's-his-name. She didn't even want to mention him.

Still, Mary's head on her shoulder was as restful to her as it was to the child, and she hated to let her off her lap when Jake and Dillon came forward.

Jake again extended his hand to help her up. "Come on in. I actually have a window air-conditioner in the living room you might enjoy. We put your bags in the cabin."

There was that smile again. "Actually, I'd like to go to the cabin and unpack. Maybe take a bath and rest. It's been a long day."

"Sure, but first come in and cool off. The cabin may be a little warm until the sun goes down. It only has overhead fans for cooling."

Reluctantly, she followed Jake and the boys into the house, noting it was very much cooler, and she felt she could breathe normally once again.

The interior was impressive with its long-beamed rafters and roughhewn side walls. The kitchen had an abundance of beautifully hand-finished cupboards with white porcelain knobs, not unlike some of the finer homes in Boston. The kitchen itself was big enough for a dance, the table enough room for twenty place settings at least. She wondered if he had planned to have more children before his wife... She shivered remembering when her own mother died. She also recalled when she was ten and how devastated she'd felt when her grandfather died. That was when she started to stutter and it made her wonder what may have caused Mary to stammer.

The sitting area was furnished with two comfortable settees upholstered in dark green fabric and an oversized wooden rocking chair with paler green cushions. Cass was surprised. She imagined a ranch house in Texas to be furnished more rustic. This one showed a definite woman's touch.

Sheer off-white drapes hung at the large widow in the bedroom off the kitchen. There were two beds and a crib, undoubtedly the girls' room. Another bedroom was toward the back of the house separate from the rest. It was a very masculine décor except for the white lace curtain at the lone window and the double bed covered with a lace coverlet over a dark green quilt.

"This is my room. The boys' rooms are upstairs."

Startled at the sudden sound of Jake's deep voice, she turned and met his gaze. "I'm sorry. I didn't hear you come in." His crystal blue eyes glistened with a ray of sunlight that peeked through the window. "Nice," she said softly.

"Pardon me?"

She quickly turned back around. "The furniture. It…it's beautiful."

"Thanks. I made it for Lilly."

"Lilly?"

"My wife."

"Oh." Cass studied the Lilies of the Valley etched in the headboard, then traced the fine lines with her fingers. "Lovely. Your whole house shows excellent craftsmanship. I've never seen such beautiful kitchen cupboards. Your wife must have been very proud."

She noted a slight shrug before Jake spoke. "Well... she was used to the finer things in life. I tried to make it as pleasant as possible."

Cass felt there was more to the story on Lilly, but since she was only a guest here, it wasn't her place to pry.

Jake stepped further into the room. She tried to maneuver by him but clumsily tripped over his boots. He caught her around the waist just in time to keep her from falling face down. She couldn't help but again feel how strong he was as he easily held her in balance.

Holding her close, he sniffed the air. "What is that smell? Your hair?"

Cass nodded. "It's me. It's lavender toilet water. Perhaps it's too strong."

"Oh, no. It smells really good. It suits you. Are you okay?" he asked without letting her go.

She breathed deeply trying to regain some composure. She felt a little dizzy with him holding her so close. He smelled musky like a man who had done a hard day's work. It was a good smell. Not at all like the men she had known in Boston with their expensive cologne splashed all over them. Jake's touch invoked a feeling she was not familiar with. It was both tantalizing and perplexing.

"I...I'm fine, thank you," she said, somehow reluctant to pull away. What in the world was wrong with her? She must have left her brain in the wagon.

Jake cleared his throat and dropped his hold on

her. "Well, if you're okay, I think I'll start supper." He laughed softly. "We're not much on cooking around here. I grill and that's about it. If I can't cook it on the grill...well, let's say we eat a lot of breakfast food and bologna sandwiches."

Cass laughed along with him. "I happen to like bologna sandwiches and I haven't had one for years. As a kid, that was my favorite snack when I came home from school. Mother always had it waiting for me." She suddenly felt very nostalgic and tears sprang to her eyes. "I'm sorry. I loved my mother so much and miss her terribly." She gazed up at him. "I'm sure your family misses their mother also."

Jake nodded. "They do," he said softly.

After grilling was finished and the table set, Cass placed napkins at each setting. The children raced to the table, yelling and shoving each other. She stood back to avoid being knocked down. She had seen street brawls in Boston that looked like a waltz compared to the Carpenters scrambling to the table. They fought over chairs and made bets on who was going to get the biggest piece of meat, or who could drink their milk the fastest or belch the loudest.

She had never heard the word "stupid" used so often in so short a time. In a matter of seconds, the twins called each other every "stupid" thing imaginable, yelling so loud the veins stood out in their neck.

Baby Faye reached and screamed for a hotdog,

while the twins stabbed each other with their forks. One of the twins called Beth a cow and she shoved him into the table, causing the iced tea to spill. Bobby pulled Mary's hair and sent her screaming to her father who seemed to handle it all with quiet resolve. Probably used to it. What chaos! She was ready to scream herself.

Jake calmly put two fingers to his lips and blew a shrill, ear piercing whistle. The children stopped dead in their tracks and stared at their father. Even Buck, who had been running around the table waiting for some scraps to fall to the ground, sat to attention and let out a soft howl.

"We'll now all take our places and bow our heads for the blessing. A—n—d," he emphasized, "remember we are privileged to have a guest sharing our food with us this evening. Let's not scare her off on her first day."

The children all turned to Cass and smiled politely. Dillon spoke softly. "Sorry about the ruckus, Miss...Cass."

Cass smiled back. "It's fine. It's been a long day and I guess children need to blow off some steam at times."

Jake motioned for Cass to take a seat at his side, then spoke softly. "We'll now all hear the blessing." He looked around the table as they all bowed their heads. "Dear Father, we thank you for the bounty before us. Let us partake of this food so it might strengthen our minds and bodies to better do Thy will. Bless this house and all who dwell here. We come to you in the name of Jesus. Amen."

Cass smiled at Jake. "That was lovely. Thank

you."

"You're welcome," he returned, then picked up a platter. "Hamburger?"

"Yes. They smell great." She took a bite. "Yum, what do you put in these to make them so tasty?"

He chuckled. "Secret ingredient. If I told you, I'd have to kill you."

"Hmmm, that's a bit drastic. I think I'll let the secret remain secret."

They both chuckled.

Except for a few giggles from the twins, the meal was finished in relative silence. The food was very tasty to everyone and Cass had never enjoyed hamburgers and chips so much.

Cass patted her stomach. "I'm so full I can barely breathe. That was delicious. I'm still trying to figure out what made those hamburgers taste so good."

Jake grinned mischievously. "I'll never tell."

Cass smiled back at him then rose and started gathering up the dirty plates.

"Oh, you don't need to do that," Jake said, taking the plates from her. "You're our guest."

"It's the least I can do. I may be here for a while and I want to do my part." She glanced at Jake. "I also know how to cook a few things my mother taught me. I'd be glad to make breakfast, lunch or dinner if you ever need me to."

Dillon stood up to help clear the table. "Hope you're here for a long time. You're a nice lady. We could use a good cook."

Beth glared at Dillon, rose, then took her dirty plate to the sink.

Cass followed Beth with her own dirty plate. "Boys," she chided, "always trying to get a rise out of us girls, huh?"

Beth gave Cass a sideward glance and poured water over the dirty dishes. "I cook just fine," she blurted defensively.

"Oh, honey, I'm sure you do. I only want to help out if needed."

"If you want to cook, then do it without me."

Cass was taken aback at the girl's hostility. So much hurt behind those dark blue eyes. So much pride in the set of her jaw. Cass decided there was no point in pursuing a conversation with the young girl at this time. Beth's attitude shouldn't be a concern to her. It wasn't like these people were going to be a part of her life forever. She would just make the best of it while she was here.

Cass loaded the dishwasher in silence and then wiped the table and put the tablecloth back on. Before she could retrieve the floral centerpiece, Jake had it in his hand and placed it on the table.

Jake glanced toward her. "You don't have to do all this."

"I know. I want to." She looked around. "Where are the kids?"

"Taking their baths and showers. Takes a while for that many taking turns even with three bathrooms."

Cass nodded knowingly, then turned to see Dillon enter the kitchen. Cass was happy to see he got the hair gel washed out. He had a comb in his hand and she instinctively took it and combed his hair in place for him, told him how handsome he was, kissed his cheek and commented on his sweet soapy smell.

Dillon smiled and hung his head down bashfully. "Thanks. I just came in to say I'm glad you're visiting us."

Jake patted the ten-year-old on the head. "Better get to bed, son. Chores come early."

Dillon gave his father a hug, turned to Cass and gave her an embarrassed wave and smiled sweetly. "Goodnight."

Cass watched Dillon leave the room then turned to Jake. "What a precious boy. He's such a gentleman."

Jake nodded. "Yep, I'm pretty proud of him." He looked her in the eyes. "You must be worn to a frazzle."

"It has been quite a day...for you, too."

"Me? I'm used to all this." He chuckled, then paused and watched her tiredly rub her hand across her neck. "Our ways aren't your ways, that's for sure, but I'll try to make your stay here as pleasant as I can."

"I know you will, Jake." Her weary gaze traveled from his feet to his head, then back to his face. A face lined from hard work and long hours in the sun. A face lined with heartbreak and struggle. A face lined with all the kindness God could grant a man.

She felt her cheeks heat when she realized she'd been studying him longer than necessary, but noted no longer than he had studied her.

He jammed his hands into his pockets and cleared his throat self-consciously. "I'll walk you to the cabin."

Cass's temperature had risen a few degrees. She turned, embarrassed at her blatant perusal of him and walked out to the porch with Jake following. "No...no need." She lifted her long hair from her neck to let the breeze cool her. "Hot tonight." She fanned herself with her other hand.

"That's Texas for you."

Buck sauntered onto the porch and sat down beside her, then licked her hand.

"Buck! Stop kissing me."

"He likes you." He looked her in the eyes. "We all do."

"Well...maybe not all."

"If you're referring to Beth, I told you, she'll come around. She was the same way with Brad while he was here building the cabin, but finally warmed up to him and even looked forward to helping him hang the curtains, etc. She's still very possessive of the way we were when her mother was alive, but I'm sure in time..."

"I hope so. She carries such a burden, trying to take on grown-up duties."

"I know. I pray about it all the time." He stepped closer. The lavender fragrance that radiated from her skin made him lightheaded. The sway of his body brought him back to earth. "Let me get you settled in." He took her arm and guided her down the porch steps with Buck trotting ahead of them.

Cass looked to the sky. "Big stars in Texas."

"Yep. Big stars, big moon, big field to plow in the morning."

Buck reached the cabin just before them, raised

his paw and opened the door.

Cass stopped, her mouth dropping open. "Buck opens doors?"

"You can thank your friend Brad for that. While he was here, he taught Buck a lot of things. They were great pals."

"Good grief. What else does he do?"

"Too many to mention tonight, but he can bring you your shoes, he can open up a cooler and bring you a cold drink, he can play dead, he can catch a Frisbee in midair to name a few."

"You left out kissing a person senseless."

"I don't think Brad taught him that. He does that on his own. Like my boys, Buck has really good taste in women." He winked and grinned.

Cass smiled and walked onto the cabin porch, turning to face Jake. "Are you flirting again?"

"Hmmm, maybe."

"Goodnight, Jake."

He saluted and smiled. "Goodnight, Cass. Sleep well." He snapped his fingers at the dog. "Come on, Buck. The lady needs her rest."

Cass watched him walk toward the house for a long moment before closing the door. Texas men were a lot different from the ones in Boston…that was for sure. She slowly turned and scanned the well-appointed room of the cabin with a comfortable bed in the corner, table and chairs, all the kitchen appliances and even a fan in the ceiling which she immediately turned on. It was a lovely room and she already felt comfortable as she made her way toward the shower to ready herself for bed.

She pulled the curtains closed, disrobed and

stepped into the tepid shower. Her skin prickled when she ran the bar of soap over it. The sensation unnerved her. Was it the water that made her feel heady, or the lingering memories of Jake's body heat when he stood so near her on the porch?

CHAPTER THREE

Cass couldn't believe how refreshed she felt upon awakening early the next morning and since she had volunteered to help with the cooking, she decided to hurry over to the house and prepare breakfast.

Some of the children were in the kitchen rubbing their sleepy eyes and searching the cupboard for breakfast food.

"Good morning, kids," Cass said cheerily. "How about I fix pancakes for everyone?" She looked at their beaming faces. "I assume you like pancakes." Dillon and the twins nodded exuberantly as did Mary. Beth stared with her usual stoic manner.

Cass asked to be shown where the flour and other ingredients were and Dillon politely pointed where everything was. She diligently went about her business and after making homemade syrup from brown sugar, they all sat down just as Jake entered the room.

"Yum, something smells good," he commented just as the twins stabbed a couple pancakes onto their plate. "Huh uh," he scolded. "Grace first. You know the rules."

Ronnie slumped his shoulders. "Ummm, thanks for...thanks for...," he thought for a long moment, then blurted, "Thanks for the food on the table."

Donnie butted in. "Now grab a fork and eat all you're able. Amen. Now can we have some pancakes?" Both twins fell into fits of giggles.

Mary clasped her hands over her face as if waiting for her father to reprimand the boys but he just shook his head and shrugged his shoulders. "I guess pancakes won out over a proper Grace."

Cass smiled and passed Donnie the platter. "You may 'eat all you're able'." Her comment brought on another round of giggles.

They all seemed to enjoy the meal Cass had made, cleaning their plates to a slickened shine.

The twins, Dillon and Jake left to go to the field to get the plowing done before it got too hot, and Beth left to do the milking while Cass cleaned the kitchen. Mary's chore was to gather the eggs and scatter feed for the chickens, geese and turkey.

After Beth returned, Cass helped her pour the milk into jugs and put them in the refrigerator, saving out a crock to let the cream rise for butter churning, Beth informed. Cass had never churned butter, but was willing to learn. Sighing, she thought to herself, *I'm certainly not in Boston anymore.*

Beth fed Baby Faye and Bobby who had finally

awakened and Mary had returned with the eggs she had gathered. Wanting to be a "big girl" Mary fixed herself a plate of leftover pancakes and asked if she could eat them on the porch so she could give Buck a bite. "He ne...never had pan...pancakes before but I thi...think he'll like them."

"My guess is that he certainly will." Cass ran her fingers through Mary's hair pushing some strands from her face. What an adorable child, she thought as sadness engulfed her thinking about the children losing their mother.

She watched Beth spoon feed the baby and give her a kiss on the cheek every time she took a bite. "You sure do love your sisters and brothers."

"More'n anybody else could ever love them," the young girl answered without looking at Cass. "I'll never leave them."

"They're very fortunate to have such a wonderful big sister as you, Beth," Cass said honestly.

Beth glanced up and for the first time Cass saw a softening in the girl's features. She appeared to be flattered by the comment.

"I mean it, truly," Cass continued.

"You do?" Beth appeared to be interested.

"Yes, of course. I'm an only child. I always wanted siblings."

"How did your Mom die?"

"She died of pneumonia."

"Oh."

Beth continued to feed Baby Faye, and Cass cut up another pancake for Bobby. "Can you say thank you?" she asked the little boy. He shook his head yes. "Then why don't you say it?" He shrugged his shoulders.

"He never talks anymore," Beth informed.

"Did he once?" Cass asked, curious.

"Just baby talk."

"Then he does have a voice?"

A long silence followed before Beth spoke again, her voice full of wonder, "If a person does a really bad thing, will they still go to heaven?"

Cass patted Beth's hand. "I like to think there's a good chance, Beth. After all, the Lord may not love the sin, but he always loves the sinner." She studied the young girl's troubled features. "You're too young to have done something 'really bad'."

"It…it's not me I'm asking for."

Just then Mary came back in with a sparkling clean plate. "Ca…ca…can I ha…ha…have another?"

Cass looked at the plate, then at Mary. "Did you clean this plate like this or did Buck?"

"Bu…buck helped."

Cass laughed. "That's what I thought." She rose and put the plate in the sink, then got a clean one from the cabinet. "One more, but eat it in here." Cass playfully yanked on Mary's sleeve. "Are we ever going to get you filled up this morning? You must have two hollow legs for all that food to go in."

Mary giggled and shook her legs to see if they were hollow.

"Do you miss your Mom?" Beth asked Cass out of the blue.

"All the time," Cass answered truthfully, then touched the locket around her neck that held her mother's picture, "but it gets so it doesn't hurt so much as in the beginning."

"I know," Beth said softly. "I'm afraid I'll forget her."

"You won't. You'll always remember her as long as you live, but it will be sweet memories."

This was the first real conversation Beth had had with her about anything personal and she didn't want to turn her away by asking too many questions.

"Would you like to see a picture of my mother?" Cass asked, snapping open the locket.

Beth leaned close and studied if for a long moment. "She looks like you," she said, then turned her attention back to feeding the baby.

"So I've been told," Cass said reminiscently, drawing the locket up to take a look herself before closing the clasp.

Beth swallowed nervously. "Some say that about me and my mother…that I look like her."

"If that is true," Cass said, "she must have been beautiful."

If Beth took it as a compliment, she didn't show it.

Cass sat quietly watching Mary finish her breakfast, then put the rest of the dirty dishes into the dishwasher before turning to Beth. "If you don't need me, I think I'll go back to the cabin and finish unpacking. I'll be back later."

While at the cabin, Cass reflected on memories of her mother who was her best friend and her father who paid too little attention to her until after her mother's death. Then he never wanted her out of his sight. It was the one reason she joined the company. She wanted to make him happy, but she doubted anything could make him happy. He was all business. Despite things he said and did, she loved him and missed him, but it also felt good to be away from the hustle and bustle of the city. She had to admit she felt free and alive. Invigorated. Even useful in a way even if it was only for a short time.

Upon returning to the house to help with lunch she discovered Beth had already fixed the three young ones a cheese sandwich and canned soup and was cleaning their dishes.

"Is there anything I can do to help?" Cass asked.

"Nope," Beth replied, methodically going about her chores. "Dad and the boys already came back, packed up their sandwiches and water jugs and went back to the field. They said they'd see us at supper."

Cass looked toward Mary who was smiling at her. "Let's play a game. We can make up poems and then sing them." Cass tried to sound cheery.

"I...I...I don't thi...think I can," Mary said sadly.

"Oh, yes you can. I'll show you how." Cass rose and took Mary's hand.

"She'll just stammer more," Beth said defensively. "When she tries to talk too much, she gets worse."

Cass walked to Beth and stroked her shoulder. The girl jerked it away.

"Listen to me, Beth. I will never do anything to make Mary's stammer worse. On the contrary. I want to help her in a way that helped my own speech defect. Singing."

Beth's eyes narrowed. "Why would you want to help her?" she snapped, then as an afterthought, "besides, how can singing help?"

"I don't know. It just does." Cass ignored Beth's rudeness. "Now come on. Let's get started." She turned her attention to Mary. "Do you know the song, 'Jesus Loves Me'?"

"I he...heard it at chur...church."

"Okay, here goes." Cass began singing and motioned for Mary to follow her lead. Surprisingly, Mary began with a stammer but before the song had ended was hardly stuttering at all and her face beamed with delight.

Beth stood with her mouth open. "How did you do that?"

"I didn't do it. Mary did it herself. I just remembered when my grandfather passed away, I stuttered for a while except when I sang. I remembered the famous country singer who stuttered when he talked but not when he sang, so I tried it and it worked. I think it will eventually work for Mary."

She turned to Bobby. "Can you sing?"

Bobby shook his head no.

"I'll bet you can," Cass said. "Maybe some time you'll sing 'Jesus Loves Me' just like Mary did."

Bobby opened his mouth and let out a high-pitched tone that would rival the highest soprano in the choir.

Beth, Cass and Mary all stared in amazement.

Cass patted Bobby's cheeks. "That's a good start."

Later that afternoon, Bobby and Mary busily played with the cats on the porch while Baby Faye sat in her highchair smearing a cookie on the tray and Cass and Beth tidied up the kitchen. Just as they finished, they heard the sound of a car horn.

Cass called to Mary, "Is someone here?"

Mary ran into the house and announced brightly. "It's Be...Be...Belle!"

As Cass and Mary went out on the porch, Bobby was jumping up and down with glee. Beth had the baby in her arms as she bolted out the door. Obviously, Belle was a very welcomed visitor.

Cass watched an extremely fetching raven-haired woman step out of the car with a basket in her hand. By the time she was halfway to the house, the children had run to meet her. Bobby reached into the basket in desperate search of something.

"Ah, ah, ah," Belle lightly scolded. "Have you been a good boy?"

Bobby nodded yes so hard Cass thought his head would snap off.

"Well then, let's see what we can find," the woman said teasingly, then conducted her own exaggerated search until she came up with a piece of hard candy. She bent down so her face was next to Bobby's. "What do I get?"

Bobby gave her a big smack on the cheek, grabbed the candy and ran back to show Cass what he had.

Cass tried to coax the boy into speaking. "You should tell the nice lady, thank you."

Bobby opened his mouth and let out that same high-pitched squeal he did before, then put the candy in his mouth and started happily hopping on one foot in a circle.

"Wow," said Belle, "that was some 'thank you'."

Cass extended her hand. "He just started that today. I'm Cass Palmer."

The woman took Cass's hand firmly. "Yes, I know."

Belle had a beautiful smile and an intriguing beauty mark just to the right of her upper lip. Cass couldn't help but wonder if it were real or, like she had seen in magazines, painted on.

A big grin spread across Belle's face. "You were the talk of the town before you came...still are for that matter."

Cass's eyebrows raised with question. "Talk of the town?"

"People wondered what you'd be like. We don't get too many visitors from up East except for Sheila and Brad once in a while." She took a deep breath. "Where's my manners? Let me introduce myself. I'm Belle Nester, a friend of the Carpenters. Thought I'd come out for a visit and see how you're doing." She laughed and added, "Quite a pile you stepped into."

Cass smiled politely and nodded agreement. "I'm only here for a little while. Kind of a vacation, I guess you'd say. As soon as I find other accommodations, I'll be moving on."

"Oh?" Belle smiled brightly.

She didn't seem upset by the news at all. In fact, Cass could have sworn she was happy about it.

"It does take a certain type of woman to like it out here...it's understandable," Belle excused kindly. "You being so young and refined and all."

Cass dropped her head and compared her blue jeans and T-shirt to Belle's shiny bright blue ruffled dress. Belle's hair was perfectly coifed in a chignon while Cass's thick hair blew every which way in the breeze. She self-consciously pushed her hair back away from her face.

For some reason, Cass didn't particularly understand the assumption Belle made that she might not be the kind of woman who could like it in Texas. "I never considered myself too refined for..."

"Oh, I wasn't insulting you. No, on the contrary. We were all rather pleased with Jake's selection. When we saw you get out of the shuttle, we thought if we couldn't have him then we wanted you to." Belle patted the back of her hair. "There will be several...uh...ladies who will be most pleased that Jake is still eligible."

For reasons Cass didn't understand, a tinge of jealousy touched her heart. "You among them?"

"Sister, I'd give the deed to a gold mine, if I had one, for a man like Jake Carpenter...but..."

"But what?"

"He wouldn't have nothing to do with the likes of me...I'm not worthy of him and I know it."

"What a thing to say. Why, you're a beautiful lady."

Belle smiled broadly. "Thanks for the 'lady'." Her smile faded reminiscently. "I've not been called a lady for years...not since Ben died."

"Ben?"

"My husband. Ben and I were headed for California. We got this far when Ben died of cancer.

I had nothing left. I couldn't go on, couldn't go back. That's when Stella took me in as one of the dancing girls."

"Stella. The woman who runs the bar?"

Belle smiled. "Yes…and while I'm not considered a 'lady' anymore by most, I'll always be grateful to Stella. I have no skills, Ben always eked out a living for us, and without him I didn't know how I was going to live." She let her breath out slowly and looked out over the pasture. "So you can see why I'd give anything to have all this…husband, children, a real home..."

Cass's gaze drifted toward the pasture along with Belle's. She understood Belle's point. She just couldn't see it for herself.

Belle turned to Cass, smiled and winked. "Don't be surprised if some of the bachelors in town come calling when they find out you're available also."

"Belle, I'm not 'available'. I'm only here for a short..."

"I know what you said, but that don't make any difference. Men are men and women are women. We're always looking."

When Bobby started chasing tom turkey, their reverie was abruptly interrupted. The bird bounded around the corner of the house toward them, gobbling in high pitch. Cass picked a long stick and pointed it at the turkey. Its claws dug into the ground to stop its momentum, the gobbling ceased and the feathered friend walked gingerly back to its place near the shed. The tom rendered one more insulting gobble which trickled to a weak cluck when it saw Cass raise the stick once more.

Belle let out a deep boisterous laugh. "My goodness, girl, you got grit. I like you Cass Palmer. I like you a lot."

Cass invited Belle to sit with her on the porch. Belle was a delightful visitor and Cass could very well see why the children were so excited when they saw her. Belle could tell the funniest stories on the townspeople and, though Cass knew no one she spoke of, her sides hurt from laughing.

"Then there was the time old Elmer Tiddle slipped in the cow dung, fell and tore the seat out of his pants on his way to church..."

"No more, Belle," Cass gasped, trying to catch her breath. "No more stories."

"It's all true," Belle relayed teasingly as if Cass doubted her. "I never made up one iota."

Their laughter dwindled to a smile, then a sigh.

In a low voice, Cass inquired, "Did you know the children's mother?"

"Lilly?" She nodded thoughtfully. "Oh, yes, we knew Lilly. God rest her troubled soul."

Cass frowned. "Troubled?"

Belle shook her head sadly. "Jake will have to tell you. It's not my place."

The children haven't talked about her much...except for Beth."

"No, I don't suppose they do. The little ones barely knew her." Belle looked out toward the field again. "So you're definitely not going to marry up with Jake?"

"No, Belle. Not me. Like I said, I'm just a guest for a short time. I'm sure he'll make one of you ladies a fine husband someday, but he's not only needing a wife, he needs a mother for his children. That certainly would take a special woman to be a mother to seven children all at once."

Belle laughed. "Seven children would be something to give pause to...but still..." She squinted to get a better view of Jake as he plowed. "What about you? No man in your life?"

"No and not interested in one."

"Aww, you never know. One might come along that tickles your fancy."

"Well, I'd love to sit all evening, Belle," Cass said changing the subject, "but I've volunteered to cook while I'm here so I'd better go in and see what's available in the kitchen to rustle up for supper before the workers get in from the field. You're welcome to eat with us."

"Only if I can help."

"Oh, no. You'll get your lovely dress soiled."

"It'll be fine. I'll just push up my sleeves. I'll chop, you cook." Belle let out another of her deep-throated laughs. "We'll get supper quicker that a cat can...blink his eye." Belle picked up the basket she brought and handed it to Cass. "Before I forget, this is from Stella. Two quarts of blackberries. Jake loves blackberry cobbler...so does Stella."

"Then I'll make sure we save a good portion for you to take back to her." Cass took the basket into the house. "I'll get the cobbler put together and while it's baking, we'll tackle the rest of the supper."

Cass glanced over her shoulder at Belle and thought what a striking woman she was. She bet if Belle tried really hard, she could win Jake over. The children already adored her. Cass continued on into the kitchen. She pictured Belle in this kitchen, in this house, in Jake's bed. Somehow that thought gave her an unexpected knot in her stomach.

Beth, Belle and Mary had a good portion of the vegetables and meat cut up for the stew by the time Cass finished the cobbler. While the stew was brewing, Cass made cornbread and coleslaw. She marveled how fresh vegetables from the garden and meat from the farm made making a meal so enjoyable.

Time flew by with Belle laughing and telling more of her stories. They didn't even hear Jake and the boys when they returned from the field.

"I smelled something good to eat every time I passed the east side with the plow," Jake said entering the house. He hung his hat on a hook by the door and wiped the sweat from his face with the sleeve of his shirt before noticing they had company.

"Hello, Jake," Belle said, a big smile beaming across her face.

"Belle! What brings you out this way?" he returned just as friendly.

"Stella's blackberries. She sent some as a welcome to your new bride...who isn't, I understand. Anyway, Stella said Cass didn't look so good the last time she saw you helping her out of the lobby. I thought I'd come out to check on her." She laughed. "No need for concern. She's a scrappy little thing, isn't she?"

Jake nodded. "I guess she could hold her own, but tell me, does everyone think I sent for a bride?"

He was clearly a little puzzled. "Cass is Sheila and Brad's good friend and she just needed a vacation from the hustle and bustle of Boston." He breathed deeply. "Boy something smells delicious and now that I've made myself clear about this bride business, let's eat."

Cass smiled. "Thank you, Jake. That was a bit embarrassing, but the delicious smell you're smelling is blackberry cobbler. I just took one out of the oven. I understand it's one of your favorites."

"You got that right." Jake went to the sink to wash his hands.

The twins made a dive for the table but Cass took them by the shoulders and guided them toward their father to wash their hands. Dillon followed suit. The young ones were already washed up and sitting quietly at the table except for Faye tapping her spoon against the highchair tray. The tapping abruptly stopped when Cass put her fingers to her lips and uttered, "Shhh."

Belle slapped the side of her leg. "By doggies if that isn't something. First that grouchy old tom turkey and now these scalawags doing your bidding and not a word exchanged...except that one old scrawny gobble from tom. You got the magic touch, girl."

They all sat down at the table and Cass said the Grace before the hungry assemblage filled their plates, then their bellies.

After a good helping of cobbler, Belle clasped her hands over her stomach. "Better not make too many visits out this way. Much more of this good cooking and I'll be losing my figure."

Cass laughed at her then scooped a large portion of cobbler into a bowl and covered it with a pie plate. "This is for Stella. You can bring the dishes back on your next visit, which I hope will be soon." She genuinely meant that. Belle was a delight to be around.

"Oh, I pop in and out quite regularly, don't I darlin'?" she said to Jake. Cass took note of the word 'darlin'. "And thanks for the cobbler, Cass. Stella will love it. I know I sure did." She turned to Jake and nodded her head toward Cass. "You're going to miss her when she leaves."

"I'll miss the cooking for sure."

Belle smiled broadly and tapped her finger against his cheek. "Is that all you'll be missing?"

Jake shook his head to ignore her innuendo. "Can I walk you to your car?"

Belle laughed at his apparent embarrassment. "Before I go, I want to let you know you're all invited to Herschel and Maude Cummins' place Preacher Sunday for a get-acquainted picnic."

"Who's getting acquainted?" Jake asked.

"Everybody…to Cass." She laughed again. "Of course, as it turns out, it'll be a 'nice-to-meet-you-have-a-safe-trip-back' picnic." She raised her eyebrows. "Unless one of our town's men tickles her fancy and she decides to stay."

Cass felt her cheeks flush and saw Jake's frown. She whispered, "Perhaps it would be better if I didn't go."

"Nonsense," Belle admonished. "It's just an excuse to have a get-together. It'll be fun. Preacher Sunday is the second Sunday of every month. He preaches in other towns some of the other Sundays. He eats at Herschel and Maude's anyway." She let out a loud cackle. "Maude thinks she has a surefire ticket to heaven through Preacher's stomach. If venison stew will do it, then she'll be there because that's what she serves him every month."

Cass chuckled. "Belle, I swear, you can come up with the most outrageous stories."

"It's true…every word. Preacher told me himself he thought he might be growing antlers," Belle added trying to be serious.

"No," Cass said, laughing so hard she could barely see.

"Come on. The Cummins live by the river and the kids love to swim there."

Cass shrugged and looked at Jake who gave her an 'it's up to you look'.

"Okay," Cass said, "what food shall we bring?"

"From what I sampled today, you bring anything you want. It'll be delicious. Well, anything but venison stew." Her words sent Cass into a giggling fit again.

Belle locked arms with Jake as he walked her to her car. Cass overheard her say to him, "Darlin' you are the most gentlemanly scalawag I've ever known…and so handsome, too." She tweaked his cheek with her well-manicured nails.

Cass watched the two as they made their way. The knot in her stomach grew tighter when Belle laughed and leaned in close to Jake, whispering something in his ear that made him lay his head back and laugh.

Why that would be of any bother to her, Cass

couldn't say. They actually made a rather striking couple and, despite Belle's occupation, she was a really nice woman. One Cass would be proud to call a friend. Then why did she feel so out of sorts seeing Belle and Jake so happy together?

Buck sauntered up beside her and let out a mournful whine then licked her hand.

She patted him on the head. "I feel the same…like I want to whine too." He licked her hand again.

"As much as I know you mean well, do you have to kiss me all the time?"

"Woof!"

"I take that as a yes." She patted his head again. "Okay, walk me to the cabin. You can open the door for me and maybe I'll share a cookie with you."

"Woof!"

CHAPTER FOUR

L ater that evening Cass sat staring at the stars out the window while Buck lay sprawled at her feet. Suddenly, Buck sprang up at the sound of a knock on the door.

Cass opened it to see Jake standing there with teary eyes.

"Am I disturbing you?" he asked.

"Is something wrong? Are the kids okay?"

"No, no. Nothing's wrong, something's right."

"Oh?"

"I cannot thank you enough for... well, Mary just sang me a song before she went to sleep. 'Jesus Loves Me'. She did not stutter. She said you taught her to do that."

"Singing helped me years ago to get over my stammering after Grandpa died. I'm glad it helped Mary. She's a sweet girl...I guess you know that." She smiled. "Come in. Buck's here just sitting around enjoying the night sky."

Jake walked in and took a seat. "Bobby's rendition of the song left a lot to be desired, however, but it's something new. As ear-piercing as it is, it's the first sound he has made since a tiny baby, so I thank you for that also."

"Bobby's singing is a work in progress," Cass returned laughingly.

Jake nodded. "Another thing I wanted to talk to you about. This thing with Belle and the others thinking you came here to marry me..."

"You don't have to explain. Although....." she smiled teasingly, "Belle seems quite taken with you."

He chuckled. "I'd have to be brain dead not to notice, but I have never encouraged that." He ran his fingers through his hair nervously. "I know that was embarrassing for you so I had to explain why you're here, but for my sake I kind of wish they continued thinking you were here for the other reason. I can't tell you how many casseroles and other culinary treats I've received from the ladies of Pine Valley since Lilly passed."

Cass couldn't help but chuckle. "They say the way to a man's heart is through his stomach. And here I made you a blackberry cobbler. Hope you don't think…"

"Of course not."

"I'm sure if you were looking for a wife, you could have your pick of any number of ladies in town…that's according to Belle."

"I'm not looking for a wife. I'm busy raising my kids to the best of my ability. I don't want to subject them to anything that might be more trauma than they have suffered."

"Jake, you are a great father. I can see that, and your children love you very much." Her eyes misted and she swiped the tears away. "My father never showed me much attention except for business, but I love him and wish him well. He was very upset with me for leaving the company and coming here."

"I'm sorry." He thought for a moment. "None of my business, but you're such an attractive, intelligent woman. Makes me wonder why someone hasn't scarfed you up."

She shook her head. "Not interested in being 'scarfed'. I'm just trying to get over a heartbreak."

"Well, you don't have to go into details, but I just want you to know that whoever he was must have been an idiot not to hang on to you."

She chuckled. It was nice to be able to laugh about it with a good friend…and Jake did seem like a good friend. "Thanks, but I was the idiot for being so blind to the whole situation."

They sat for a long time both staring out the window at the moon before Jake spoke.

"Come on, Buck, let's get out of here so the lady can get some rest." He rose along with Cass and she walked him to the door. "Thanks again, Cass, for what you did for Mary."

Without giving it too much thought, she put her arms around his shoulders and gave him a hug, knowing she held on longer than she had intended. She felt him hug back and pull her close to him.

When they parted, he looked her in the eyes for a long moment and leaned forward almost touching her lips with his but abruptly pulled back, let his breath out and whispered, "Goodnight, Cass, sleep well."

After closing the door, she leaned against it to steady her trembling heart. That was close, so close she could almost feel his lips on hers. A feeling came over her she had not felt before. "Have I gone mad?" She looked to the heavens. "God, I need your strength and guidance. I don't want anyone to get hurt over some flirtatious happening---not the kids, not Jake and selfishly, not me. Amen."

Early the next morning before dawn, she woke with snoring going on behind her back. She froze. Who was in bed with her? Jake? A hug is one thing but I hope he didn't get the impression he could... She turned quickly, ready for combat, when a big hairy face lifted and licked her cheek.

"Buck!" He licked her again. "Stop that!" She reminded herself to chastise Brad for teaching the dog to open doors.

She grabbed her cell phone and dialed Sheila.

"Hello," came a sleepy voice.

"It's Cass."

"You okay?"

Cass could hear Sheila yawning. "Sorry to call at such an ungodly hour but this has been a rather enlightening two days here in Texas."

"So you arrived. I wondered how your trip was."

"The trip was…well, a trip, but there are a few things you omitted when you suggested I come here for rest and relaxation. Actually, rest and relaxation is kind of a joke. Why didn't you tell me Jake had seven kids?"

"Would you have gone if I had?"

"Probably not."

"That's my answer."

"About the only thing you were right about is that Jake is a nice person. He is, I'll give you that, but he has enough to take care of here with kids, chores and about a hundred animals. He sure didn't need another person on the farm." She turned to Buck who had gone back to sleep and was snoring again. "Speaking of animals, guess who was in bed with me this morning?"

"Who?" Sheila sounded very awake and interested.

"A big hairy dog, that's who."

"Awwww, Buck. I love that dog. He's the greatest. I miss him."

"Did you know he opens doors by himself?"

"Oh, yeah, isn't that amazing. Brad taught him that."

"And I'm going to choke Brad when I see him." She took a short breath. "Sheila, I need to leave here and there is no place to go. No hotel rooms to be had and you know I can't go back to Boston, unless I move in with you."

"About that. You know how much I love you but I will probably be moving soon. Rob and I have taken our relationship to another level. We're talking marriage in a few months. Of course, I want you back to be my maid of honor."

"Oh, Sheila, I'm so happy for you." She

chuckled. "About marriage. The townspeople all think I am a mail order bride or something. They thought I came to marry Jake. They're even having a get-together of all the church people as a get-acquainted party for me. One of the ladies from town came out to meet me and when I told her I wasn't here to marry and become an instant mother to seven, she was relieved and said lots of other women in town would be so happy, not to mention bachelors who would be interested in me since I'm available also. Where would they get such an idea that Jake and I were going to marry?"

"Hmmm, well stranger things have happened."

"What?" Cass let her breath out hastily. "Wait! What have you done? You're my best friend. How could you do this to me? Is Jake in on this? Is that why he's so nice and accommodating to me?" Then to herself, *and almost kiss me.*

"Hey, hold it a minute. Do what?"

"Isn't this a fix-up? You and Brad are in cahoots. Is that why you didn't tell me about seven kids? You were trying to find a mate for Jake."

"Stop it, Cass. You're getting all worked up for nothing. Brad and I were not 'fixing' you up for crying out loud. We did think it would be good for you to see what a real, honest, trustworthy man is like so you wouldn't be so bitter against men like you were the last few months in Boston."

"Okay, I believe you. It's just been a rather busy couple of days with all the kids and animals, etc."

"I know the twins can be a handful, but Dillon kind of makes up for them. Beth is a little distant but hope she's getting more social. The others are just sweet, little children."

"You're right. All are adorable. Jake says Beth will come around one of these days. She has taken on too much responsibility for the younger ones, I think, but she refuses help. I did cook breakfast yesterday and supper later they all seemed to enjoy."

"Yum, wish I were there. I know your cooking."

"Well, I'll let you get back to sleep. Just wanted you to know I got here okay, but will be looking for other accommodations as soon as I find out where they are."

"Oh, friend, give it a chance. I think it's good you have things to do to get your mind off...you know...him."

"Thanks, dear friend. Tell Brad I hate him." She then laughed. "I still can't believe this dog opens doors and gets in bed with people."

Sheila laughed too. "He likes you."

"Ya think?"

They said their goodbyes and air kissed each other before Cass leaned back on her pillow for a few minutes, hoping Sheila told her the truth — that this was not an intentional match-making ploy on her and Brad's part. She then poked Buck with her elbow. "Get up, you lazy hound. Might as well go to the house and get started on breakfast."

Buck stayed in bed watching Cass dress and comb her hair, then eagerly leaped to the floor, tail wagging, and followed her to the house.

She saw Jake sitting on the porch, a carafe of coffee and two mugs on a side table. He patted a chair beside him and poured her a cup of coffee.

"Thought you'd be coming up here soon. I just got an early call from Sheila."

"I'm sorry. That's my fault. I got her out of bed, but waking up to Buck in bed with me and thinking it was... a person, kind of rattled my brain. I instinctively called Sheila to protest her brother teaching Buck how to open doors. There is no lock on the door."

"I know. While Brad was here building the cabin, Mary locked herself in the bathroom and didn't know how to unlock it. We had to break the latch to get her out...so, no, there are no locks on any doors around here. Sorry."

Jake cleared his throat. "I understand you thought Sheila and Brad instigated our meeting each other for reasons other than a vacation. If they did, I want you to know I had nothing to do with that."

"She said they didn't, but..."

"She said stranger things have happened."

"She said those exact words to me. That's why I thought..."

"I know. I did too, but she finally convinced me it was not their intent, although I think that would be something they might do. They want me to 'put myself out there' as they say, but I'm not ready for that." He looked at her sadly. "I don't want you to leave. I feel like it's my fault. Last night I was so overwhelmed with gratitude for what you did for Mary, I lost control for a second and almost..."

"I know. But you didn't and that is not why I need to leave. You have too much on your hands with the kids and chores, I don't want to upset your life or the kids' lives."

"I know this has not turned out as you had planned for a vacation, but you are more than welcome to stay. You don't have to cook or do anything you don't feel like doing."

"Stop." She took a sip of coffee. "As long as I do stay, I want to help out. I love to cook, I love interacting with the kids and helping any way I can. I do have a teaching degree so if they need help academically..."

"I just don't want you to think you're a burden."

She smiled. "You do have your hands full around here. I just never thought about how much work there is to run a farm. I admire you so much for all you do."

"This place belonged to my parents. I was living in California going to college on a scholarship. I had met Lilly, we married and thought we'd be settling down there, but Dad passed away of cancer suddenly and I came back to help Mom and the hired hands. Lilly didn't take to it so well, but by then Beth was on the way and we both loved the idea of having a baby."

"It must have all worked out. You had several more."

"Yes, we certainly did, but that's another story." His demeanor turned sad. "Mom died just a few months after we arrived. I really think she died of a broken heart. She and Dad were like one heart in two bodies. I've never known such a perfect couple — so in love. That's what I want."

"Sounds wonderful. I think we all want that." To change the subject, she mentioned, "I never see hired hands around."

"Oh, I have them when needed. Actually, the boys and I handle the day-to-day work just fine." He chuckled. "Keeping them busy keeps them out of trouble. Most of the time."

"I think they're terrific boys."

He smiled and nodded. "Right now, there's another matter I'd like to discuss with you. It's about the Preacher Sunday thing. I don't want you to feel uncomfortable if some of the men…"

"I know. Belle told me. You're right. It might have been better if they thought what they thought. At least for now."

"I was thinking the same thing." He filled their cups and took a sip. "What would you think about letting them think we're, I don't know, getting better acquainted and seeing what transpires."

"Oh, Jake, I don't like living a lie. What about the kids? I wouldn't want them to think we're anything but friends of friends."

"We could just say we were playing a game…maybe so many of the ladies wouldn't bring all those casseroles out here and men wouldn't be visiting you."

"Jake, you know this is a crazy idea. Maybe Dillon and Beth would understand but the little ones?"

"We won't be acting on our farce. It will just be in front of the people at the Preacher's Sunday thing. It might deter some of the traffic that I know will be coming our way. Knowing Belle, word has already gotten out that we are up for grabs."

Cass stared at the sunrise just coming up and finished her second cup of coffee. "I don't know,

Jake. Let me think about it."

"That's all I ask. Think about it. After all, stranger things have happened, I've heard."

She glared at him. "If I hear that expression one more time today, I'll scream."

His laughter prompted Buck to come bounding up on the porch and jump into Cass's lap nearly knocking her over and giving her a "kiss" on the cheek.

Still laughing, Jake snapped his fingers. Buck jumped down and sat obediently staring at one then the other.

"That dog is going to be the death of me yet," Cass said, letting her breath out in a huff.

"He likes you."

"Too much."

"I told you, he has good taste in women." Jake laughed again. "Of course his morals leave a lot to be said, crawling in bed with a woman he barely knows."

Cass couldn't help but break into laughter herself, giving Jake a friendly punch in his shoulder. "It is so fun to genuinely laugh again, Jake. Thanks."

"Don't thank me. I need to be thanking you. I haven't enjoyed a woman's company like this for a long time. You know — with no strings attached."

Cass smiled. "Definitely, no strings attached."

"Although," Jake added playfully, "stranger things..."

"Do you want another punch in the shoulder?"

They both broke into laughter.

Breakfast of scrambled eggs, sausage, toast and jelly was enjoyed by all in a jolly manner. Even Beth smiled a couple of times at her father's silliness. Cass couldn't help but feel good about being on the farm. Maybe it was just because it was a new thing, maybe it would get old and tedious. Then again, maybe not.

After cleaning the kitchen with Beth's help, Cass and Mary sang their song again and Mary got better and better. Cass marveled at what a beautiful voice Mary had. She made a mental note to tell Jake to encourage Mary to sing more…maybe at church. Bobby did his usual squeal and Cass tried to get him to say 'Jesus', but all he did was screech, and often, while she and Mary sang.

"Mary's doing so well, don't you think, Beth?"

Beth glanced at them and nodded. "I guess. Who could hear over Bobby's yelling? It was better before when he didn't make a sound."

Cass smiled. "Well, maybe it will mellow out in time. Let's hope."

She rose to leave when Faye reached her arms toward her and said, "Mama." It stunned her for a moment.

Beth hurried to the baby and grabbed her out of the chair. "That is not your Mama," she blurted.

Cass turned to Mary and Bobby. "Sweeties, take this leftover sausage and go out on the porch. I'm sure Buck is waiting for some breakfast."

They left in silence, with Mary looking back frowning. Cass knew she must be puzzled by Beth's outburst.

The baby started to cry, still reaching for Cass. "She's just a baby, Beth. She doesn't know any better. Don't upset her." Cass took the baby from her. Faye immediately stopped crying.

"You are not our mother."

"I know that, you know that, Faye doesn't know what she's saying. I have no idea why she called me that. Has she ever called anyone Mama?"

"No. After our mother died, I told her I was her Mama now. She didn't even know our mother, and she's never even called me that."

"Well, maybe she was calling out to you."

"She reached for you."

She knew Beth wanted to protest more, but Cass ignored her and took the baby to the living room, sat in the rocker and rocked her to sleep. While there, Cass went over in her mind what Jake had suggested about them pretending to be more than acquaintances. She could see that Beth would not take to the idea even if she knew it was just a game. She'd tell Jake this evening when she got him alone that it just would not work no matter how good their intentions were. She was not about to upset Beth's world any more than it was.

That evening after an enjoyable dinner and all the children were bathed and in bed, Cass and Jake sat on the porch relaxing and drinking iced tea.

"Thanks again for the delicious supper. You're a wonderful cook." Jake playfully rubbed his full stomach.

Cass smiled. "It's what I like to do...cook."

"You do it so well." He hesitated before continuing. "Beth seemed a little more out of sorts tonight. Do you know what that was all about? She hardly spoke a word."

Cass took a long breath, then let it out. "Yes, I do know. Today Faye reached for me and called me 'Mama'. Beth went all to pieces and yelled at the baby that I was not her Mama and told me in no uncertain terms that I was *not* their mother. Faye started crying so I took her in the other room and rocked her to sleep. I tried to console Beth and told her I was not trying to be anything but a friend."

"I'm sorry. I'll speak to Beth. Her demeanor is uncalled for."

"No, don't, Jake. Beth has problems with me being here. I've tried to convince her I'm only trying to help her with the little ones, but she just won't accept that." She sipped her tea, then said, "What you proposed we do about making others think we're striving to be a couple just won't work. Beth would never consent to that and I don't want to upset her any more than I have."

Jake took her glass from her and put it on the side table along with his, then took her hand. "It's not you, Cass. Believe me, Beth has issues with all women who come here with their casseroles and try sweet-talking me and the kids."

"She seems to like Belle."

"Because she knows I have no feelings for Belle, but at first she treated her just like she's treating you. When Beth understands we are 'just friends', she'll be okay. I promise."

"I don't know. I still feel like I should find other accommodations."

He pulled her up from her chair. "Come, I'll walk you to the cabin. Get a good night's sleep. We'll talk about this tomorrow."

Buck ran ahead of them and, of course, opened the door.

As Jake and Cass stood in the opened doorway, he said, "I'll let Buck in the house tonight. He won't mind sleeping in the twins' room. He won't bother you."

Cass looked down at the dog. "He looks kind of sad."

"I'd be sad, too, if I had to be away from you." He pulled her into an embrace.

"Jake...don't."

He immediately stepped away. "I'm sorry. It's just that I do enjoy your company and absolutely do not want you to leave."

She hung her head, patted Buck, and then looked back at Jake. "Okay, I'll stay for a while longer and see how it goes." A large grin spread across her face. "I sure don't want to upset Buck by leaving."

Jake smiled back. "I knew that dog would come in handy one of these days. If he can make you stay, I'll give him extra people food from now on."

"You're crazy, Jake Carpenter."

"Crazy over you."

"Mmmm, are you flirting again?"

"Is it working?"

She put her hand on his cheek. "Maybe, a little."

"Then it seems pretty easy to me that we could

pull off the game I suggested? I'll talk to the kids. If it's okay with them, is it okay with you?" He took her hand from his face held it tightly. "You know something? I don't know why Faye would call you Mama, but it sounds a little like some scheming on somebody's part…maybe two somebodies."

Cass thought a moment. "The twins?"

"I'm pretty sure that is something they would do. They are the ones who asked if you were going to be their 'Ma' when you first arrived. Remember?"

"I do."

"Don't worry about Beth. As soon as I get the truth out of those rascals, I'll tell Beth. She knows her brothers and it might ease her feelings a little. Then I'll explain the 'game' again."

"Make sure the kids are okay with it. Then we'll talk."

He pulled her into his arms and hugged her tightly while Buck whined and squeezed in between them.

Jake stepped back and glared at Buck. "You jealous mutt!"

Cass pointed to the dog. "My hero. Rescuing me from this flirtatious man."

They were both still laughing as Jake and Buck sauntered toward the house. Cass's laugh dwindled to a smile as she thought. What if Buck had not intervened? Would the friendly hug have blossomed into something more…and would she have wanted it to? Of course not…well, maybe.

CHAPTER FIVE

The next few days were a blur of activity. Cooking, cleaning, singing with Mary, and teaching Beth how to braid Mary's hair.

While tying a bow at the end of the braid, Beth turned to Cass. "Preacher Sunday is in two days."

"I know. You have any idea what food we can fix to take?"

"I don't care about that. I want to know if you and Dad are going to act like married people in front of them."

Cass put her arm around Beth's shoulders. "No, not like married people. Just play like we are becoming more than friends so they will know we are not 'available' as Belle said."

"Are you?"

"Are we what, honey?"

"Are you becoming more than friends?"

Cass thought a long moment. "That can't

happen. I'll be leaving one of these days. I need to get on with my life...maybe get a teaching job back in Boston."

"I know Dad likes you. Dillon thinks so too."

Cass smiled. "I like your dad too. We have a lot of fun together." She looked seriously at Beth. "But fun and games is not love. You want your father to be in love with someone, not just like. Someone who will love him *and* you kids and love to be there for all of you." Her mind drifted off into reverie. "By the way, did your dad tell you why Faye called me Mama?"

"The twins are creeps. They admitted the other morning when they were playing with Faye on the porch, they pointed to you through the kitchen window and called you Mama several times until Faye did the same. If that was their idea of a joke, it isn't funny."

"Well, I wouldn't go so far as to call them creeps, but I'm glad you don't think I had anything to do with it. I'll try to train Faye to call me Cass."

"Okay, but I guess I can't tell the difference between your 'like' with my dad and his 'like' with you and 'love'."

Cass put her arm across Beth's shoulders. "You're one smart cookie. You'll know the difference when you're older."

Beth turned and walked away pulling Mary with her as she walked out the door. "Maybe. But maybe I know now." She glanced back. "Another thing I know is that no matter how much my dad 'likes' you, you will go away just like..." She stopped short and left.

At least Beth was talking to her, but she hoped the girl had not come to any conclusions about the 'game' she and Jake were playing for Preacher's Sunday. Cass didn't want Beth to think she would intentionally cause her dad to have more than 'like' for her then just leave. Her mind went back to the old saying about deceiving being a tangled web.

Later that afternoon, Cass and the twins played catch in the front yard. Buck leaped and tried to catch the ball as they threw it to each other. Cass laughed so hard she could hardly catch the ball with Buck jumping on her. One of the twins ran over to Cass and pushed Buck away and gave Cass a big hug around her waist.

The other twin called loudly, "Ronnie, get back over here. We are supposed to be trying to beat her at catch. Don't be buttering up to her."

So this one was Ronnie. She noted a small mole on the top of his left ear and wondered if Donnie had one two. If not, she'd be able to tell them apart.

"Go on back to your brother. If I catch your throw three more times and you guys miss one, I win."

She won, but they all laughed and ran up on the porch and plopped down in the chairs to catch their breath.

"I got an idea," she said. "When Bobby wakes from his nap, why don't you guys try singing 'Jesus Loves Me' for him? Maybe if he hears a boy's voice, he won't scream so."

"Good luck with that," Donnie said. "When he hears Ronnie sing, he'll run for the hills."

Ronnie stuck his tongue out at his brother. "You should talk. You sound like a fog horn."

"Boys, stop fussing. Do this for me. Let's just see if it works."

"You asked for it," they both said.

"Thank you. I'm sure you both sing beautifully. Now how about I go in and bring us out some cookies I baked and some drinks."

Their smiles told her that was the best idea she had.

Cookies eaten, drinks drank and both boys had laid their heads against Cass and fallen asleep. They were such rowdy boys while awake she knew, but asleep against her shoulders, they were angels. Looking down at them, she noted Donnie did not have the tell-tale mole. She smiled knowing they would not be able to fool her again.

Bobby came out on the porch, rubbing sleep out of his eyes. He looked at the one cookie left on the plate and pointed at it.

"Yes, you may have it, sweetie. But first you must promise me something."

He raised his brows in question, but took the cookie just as the boys roused.

"Okay," she said cheerily, "now that we are all here, let's get started." She turned to Bobby. "You, my dear boy, are going to sing with the twins. No screeching, just singing. Can you say, Jesus?"

Bobby shook his head no.

"I know you can if you try." She began to sing the song and motioned for the twins to join her.

As they sang, Bobby stared at first one, then the other, while finishing his cookie. When done, he climbed on Cass's lap and touched her lips with the tips of his fingers.

"Sing with us, Bobby," Ronnie said, "so we can get back to playing ball."

After several minutes into their songfest, Bobby opened his mouth wide and bellowed in a very low tone, "Jeeeesus woves meeeeee."

Cass hugged him and rocked back and forth with glee. "You did it, Bobby. You sang the song." He smiled proudly and blurted out again, "Jeeeesus woves meeeee."

"Satisfied?" Donnie asked Cass. "You've created a monster. Now he'll never stop singing."

"I hope not," she answered. "I think it's the first step to Bobby communicating with us."

The twins ran off the porch and began playing ball as Bobby sang his heart out loud and clear just as Jake and Dillon came in from their workday.

"What's this?" Jake asked, lifting Bobby up and giving him a kiss on the cheek.

Cass grinned. "He's learning to sing with the twins, and I'm sure it will get better with time."

"Let's pray it does," Dillon laughed.

After supper she found herself again on the porch with Jake after the kids were in bed.

"We need to talk," she said.

"I don't like the sound of that."

"Beth thinks you like me and not just like like."

"She said something?"

"Yes, she asked if we were going to 'play like we're married' at Preacher's Sunday. I told her we were only going to act like we were getting better acquainted."

"And?"

"She didn't buy it. Jake, I hate that we are upsetting her. Not only her, but she said Dillon feels you might be 'liking' me. I assured her that we do like each other as friends, but she still seemed upset by that prospect when she knows I'll be leaving one of these days."

She watched Jake study his hands for a long time before he spoke. "I do like you, Cass."

"Jake..."

"Hear me out. I don't know if it's because my best friends are your best friends, but I feel I've known you for a long time, not just a couple weeks. I heard a lot of nice things about you from Sheila long before she suggested you come for a vacation."

"I'd be telling a lie if I said I didn't feel the same way. I also heard so much about you from Sheila and Brad that I felt I already knew you...except for seven kids and a zoo."

He laughed and took her hand and squeezed it. "Sorry that all came as a shock to you, but I'm so glad you're here. Look what you've done for Mary and Bobby already and teaching Beth how to braid hair. That in itself is a great feat. I feel Beth is coming out of her shell. Cass, you will make a wonderful teacher. I wish you nothing but the best of life doing whatever makes you happy, wherever it may be. You deserve happiness."

Tears sprang to her eyes. "That is so kind of you, Jake. I've actually never known a kinder man than you. The way you treat your children, your animals, me..." She smiled at him and put her hand to his cheek. "All that and so much more. Not too bad to look at either. I agree with Belle, you are one handsome cowboy."

He kissed the palm of her hand. "Are you flirting with me, Miss Palmer?"

"Probably. You taught me well."

"Good for me. At least I did something right."

"Before this gets all sickeningly sweet, I think I'll retire to the cabin."

"I'll walk you."

"I think it might be better if you stay here."

"You're probably right. I'm in one of those flirty moods."

She shook her finger at him. "Shame on you."

"I'll let Buck walk you home if you feel that way."

"You put Buck in the twins' room. I'll see you at breakfast. I'm planning on cinnamon toast, ham and cheese omelets and coffee…lots of coffee."

"My kind of woman."

"So I've noticed."

He laughed again. "Awww, you could have said I was your kind of man."

She waved as she walked across the lawn. "Coulda, shoulda, woulda. Goodnight."

Sleep did not come easily. She could not quit thinking about what was happening between her and Jake. Sure, it was fun to kid around with him and genuinely laugh for the first time in a long time. Even though she barely had time for the "rest and relaxation" she had come for, she felt uncommonly "rested and relaxed" when she was with Jake and his family. Too be totally honest, she needed to be very careful not to cause worry for the children, Beth especially.

Breakfast was a big hit with all, and the boys left to do their daily chores and cleaning out the horse stalls. Cass smiled when she saw Bobby tagging along. She expected him to start singing any moment…and he did. That made both she and Beth laugh and shake their heads.

While clearing the table, Faye started singing also. Beth and Cass looked at each other and raised their brows. "Is that 'Jesus Loves Me' in baby talk?" Beth asked.

"Hard to tell. They didn't teach baby talk in college," Cass said laughing as she picked Faye out of her highchair and gave her a hug and kiss on the cheek. "So pretty, Faye. Maybe you kids can sing that at church some Sunday." She pointed to herself. "Can you say my name? Cass?"

Faye put her hand on Cass's cheek. "Cass Mama."

"Sorry about that, Beth. We'll have to work on that later." She smiled at the baby. "Still it would be nice if all the kids sang their song at church."

Beth said, "It would have to be when Dad preaches."

Cass looked puzzled. "Your Dad is a pastor?"

"Yeah, when Preach is away."

"You call your Preacher, Preach?"

"He doesn't like his first name so he wants to be called Preach."

"What's his first name?"

"Marian. He thinks it sounds too much like a girl's name."

"It can be both, but getting back to your dad. He's a preacher?"

Beth looked at her sternly. "You don't think my dad can preach?"

"Oh, no, Beth. I didn't mean it that way. It's just that he has never mentioned it. I actually think that's wonderful and can't wait to hear him," she said truthfully.

"Preach will be giving the sermon tomorrow before the get-acquainted party, but maybe you'll hear Dad next Sunday…that is if you're still here."

Cass noted Beth eyed her suspiciously. "I'm sure I'll be here another week." Then to change the subject, she said smilingly, "Speaking of the party, how about we all dress up for it?"

"I don't have a party dress." Beth looked aside. "My mother had a bunch of those."

Cass felt a sadness engulf her heart. "What happened to them?"

"Some are in my closet. She gave them to me before she..."

"Come, let's take a look."

She, Beth, Mary and Faye left the kitchen and

went to Beth's room where they found a beautiful royal blue dress hanging in Beth's closet.

"This color would be beautiful on you, Beth," Cass said holding the dress up to the girl's shoulders.

"Too much foo-foo for me."

"Only the puffy sleeves, which I can fix," Cass offered.

"How?"

"Well, do you have needle and thread?"

Beth nodded and pointed to the bottom drawer of the dresser.

"Perfect," Cass said taking the scissors and other sewing equipment out. She noted there was a box to the side. "What's in here?"

"Nothing important."

Cass, without thinking, shook the box and heard it rattle. "Sorry. Hope I didn't break anything."

Beth took the box from her and opened it. "Everything's okay."

Cass noted it was full of beads, twine, and ribbon. "Your mother made jewelry?"

Beth shook her head. "Hardly. That's my stuff."

"Oh, honey, why did you stop? These beads are beautiful. Can you show me something you've made?"

Beth took a deep breath, sat Faye down on the bed with Mary, then went to her closet and reached for a jewelry box on the top shelf. She opened it to an array of bracelets and necklaces and pulled out one to show Cass. "I made this for my mother but she never wore it."

Cass took it from her and examined it carefully.

"It is so beautiful. Why wouldn't she wear such a wonderful gift?"

Beth hung her head. "She said she didn't wear costume jewelry. She only wore genuine jewels---diamonds, emeralds, rubies---that kind of stuff."

"I'm so sorry." She smiled. "Maybe we can find something for you to wear tomorrow with the dress we are going to alter to fit you."

Beth pulled the bracelet from her and put it back in the case. "No. I don't want to."

Cass didn't pursue it any further. She surmised it reminded Beth too much of her mother. "Okay then, let's get started on the dress. First, we'll take the sleeves out and make it more of a youthful sundress. Probably shorten it for a more flattering look for a young girl."

Beth stared at the dress. "You can do that?"

"I can and you won't even know it's the same dress."

Beth shrugged her shoulders, picked up Faye and took a seat beside the bed. When Faye fell asleep, Beth put her in her crib for a nap. Mary sat on the bed watching the alterations while she softly sang, 'Jesus Loves Me'.

A couple hours later, the dress was finished except for pressing. It fit Beth perfectly and Cass could tell by the expression on Beth's face when she looked in the mirror that she was very pleased.

"Let's keep this our secret, Beth, from the rest. I want to see their faces when they see how beautiful their big sister is all dressed up for Sunday."

Beth's smile told it all. "There's a steamer in the closet. You won't have to iron the wrinkles out. The steamer does it for you."

"Great. That's what I use at home when possible. I hate to iron."

Beth laughed so hard she bent over. "I do too. I make Dillon do it."

Mary stopped singing and laughed with them, then doing the sing-song like Cass had taught her, she said, "Caaan I wheeere my piiink dress tooomorrow?"

Cass sang back, "Youuuu certainlyyyy maaay."

They were still chuckling when they went to the kitchen to make lunch. It was the first time Cass felt at ease with Beth and she felt so blessed to have pleased the young girl.

The rest of the day went by as usual with cooking, eating, cooking again, eating again. Every once in a while, Beth and Cass would glance at each other and smile.

"What's going on with you two?" Jake said to Cass after supper.

"What two?"

"Don't be coy."

"Nothing. What would be 'going on'?"

"I don't know. Probably my imagination."

"Probably. What's going on with you?"

"Me? I never have anything 'going on'. No time for 'goings on'."

"How about preaching? Beth told me."

"Oh, is that what you call 'going on'. Yes, I'm the interim pastor when Preach is absent."

"You mean Pastor Marian?"

That brought on giggles from the children.

"Please," Jake told them, "never ever call him that. He hates it. We could all end up as Satan's roommates for that."

"Okay, we wouldn't, Dad," Dillon said.

"I know you kids wouldn't, but I don't know about our illustrious visitor from Boston."

"Ooooo, 'illustrious'. I haven't been called that since....never." She laughed then pointed to the baby. Faye was falling asleep in her chair and Bobby was getting droopy eyed.

"Okay, I think it's time for baths and bed," Jake ordered.

Cass nodded. "You go ahead and help them. I'll clean up here. I'll see you all in the morning...early. We have a lot of getting ready for church and the get-acquainted party. I've already baked a chocolate cake to take. I hid it in the cupboard so none of you guys would be tempted to sneak a piece."

Jake and the boys moaned. "You think we'd do something like that?" Jake said.

"I do."

"You're right."

"Also," Cass continued, "I hope all you men dress in your finest for the occasion. You don't want us girls to outshine you." She winked at Beth as they passed each other.

Jake put his hand on her arm. "Wait for me. I'd like to talk...please."

How could she reject his request when he had such a handsome face pleading with her? "Of course, maybe a minute or two."

He nodded and she noted that blue-ribbon smile of his that made her feel like falling into his arms. A mental slap brought her to her senses. The man wants to talk. What's so wrong with that?

Later as they sat together on the porch admiring the starlit sky, Jake turned to her. His expression so serious it gave her pause. "Is something bothering you?" she asked.

"Not really. I just don't want you to think I don't take pastoring seriously because I… what do we call it…flirt with you on occasion."

"No, I was just surprised you were a preacher. I actually think that's wonderful." She smiled. "And I don't think that 'flirting' is only one-sided."

"Hope not." He smiled back. "Preachers do flirt with those he likes a lot."

"But..."

"Oh, no. I hate 'buts'."

"I was just going to say, we need to keep it fun and games. For the kids' sake."

"Is it only fun and games?" He studied her face for an answer.

She hesitated momentarily. "Jake, as much as I do like you, we *have* to keep it fun and games. It can't be more. I will eventually be leaving. I'll have to get on with my life. I do really plan on a teaching career." She patted him on the hand. "To be honest, the longer I stay, the harder it is going to be to leave."

"You don't have to tell me that. I have nightmares about your leaving."

"Don't Jake." She felt like crying.

"Too late."

She rose. "I'm going to the cabin. Sleep well, no nightmares. I'm not leaving for a while."

"That's nice to know. I was afraid I might be running you off telling you the truth about my feelings for you." He stood to stand beside her. "You're an amazing woman and I'd be crazy not to think a lot of you, but I know you'll be leaving. I don't have any doubts about that. My feelings for you does not make me want you to give up your dreams for the future." He pulled her close to him. "But you're right. We need to keep it fun and games in front of the kids. I don't want them to become so attached to you — and some are already — that they will be devastated when you go. I'm a grown man, I might be able to get over you being gone, but they wouldn't. They've lost a lot already. Soooo, no strings attached."

She could feel his heart beat against her shoulder. "I agree. The kids come first. And, yes, no strings attached."

He looked down on her face. "But for tonight…" He brought his lips gently to hers.

Her knees weakened and she nearly collapsed. Reluctantly pulling away from his embrace, she whispered, "That kiss, as wonderful as it was, cannot happen again. Please."

"Sorry if I took advantage of —"

"No, you didn't. I think I wanted it just as much as you did, but we can't show that kind of affection in front…"

"I know. It won't happen again." He walked her down the steps. "You go on to the cabin, have a good night's sleep and I'll see you early in the morning. I won't say the kiss never happened, but I will try to behave myself around you."

"Is that a promise?"

"Maybe, maybe not."

She chuckled. "Jake, you're impossible."

"I know, but I'm hoping 'impossible' grows on you." He smiled broadly. "Has it a little?"

"Mmmm, maybe, maybe not."

She heard him laughing as she walked toward the cabin. Unfortunately, yes, impossible has definitely grown on her, but that will be her secret.

Speaking of secrets, she called out, "It just dawned on me why your hamburgers tasted so good…just like tacos. You put cumin on them."

"Busted!" She heard him laughing. "I didn't even know what that was. I thought I was putting pepper on them until it was too late."

"Could you fix them like that again?"

"You know what they say, 'Stranger things have happened'."

She doubled up her fist and waved it in the air at him and yelled as she entered the cabin. "One of these days, Jake Carpenter!" The last sound she heard was his taunting laugh.

CHAPTER SIX

Church service was a combination of a rousing sermon from 'Preach' to squirming youngsters and loud singing from Bobby who sang his rendition of 'Jesus Loves Me' no matter what the congregation was singing. It was an embarrassment to Beth who sat prim and proper in her seat with Faye beside her who was tearing the program into tiny pieces. Mary sat quietly beside Cass holding her hand. The twins were sitting in the pew behind them and Jake had to turn to them every once in a while to quiet their whispering. The only real gentleman in the group was Dillon who seemed glued to what Preach was saying.

Cass was so impressed how they all looked in their Sunday best, especially Beth whom Jake had made a big fuss over when he saw her. She had actually given Cass the credit for making her look like that. Cass felt so blessed that when they made the alter call, she went up to thank God for all he had given her these last weeks. No matter what happened, she would never forget the joy she felt being here.

As they exited the church, Preach was at the door to shake everyone's hand and invite them to the get-acquainted party. Pointing to Cass he told them she was a guest of honor. Belle tried to interrupt him, saying maybe there was a mistake, but Jake caught her by the arm and whispered, "Things have changed. You might have been right in the first place. We're getting more acquainted and becoming really good friends."

Belle smiled, "Mmmm, will there be wedding bells ringing in the near future?"

Cass said, "Uh, we haven't gotten to that point yet."

"This is Belle you're talking to. Who you kidding? I see how you two look at each other."

Jake grabbed Belle by the arm and said, "Come on. Let's get to the party before all of Preach's venison stew is eaten up."

Belle whispered loud enough for Cass to hear. "That might be more of a blessing than the sermon today." All three laughed softly.

At the party, a gentleman named Homer latched onto Cass. She was afraid maybe word had not gotten out about her not being available, but all he wanted was how she made her blackberry cobbler. She laughed, relieved and gave him step by step instructions which he said he could remember without writing it down. He gave her a thank you hug and whispered his reason for wanting to make a cobbler. She smiled and patted him on the cheek wishing him good luck.

She walked back to where Jake was standing looking solemn.

"You and Homer seem to be hitting it off nicely," he said soberly.

She smiled up at him. "Jealous?"

"Don't want him to think he has a chance with you. Not while I'm around."

She tapped him on the cheek. "Why, Mr. Carpenter, you *are* jealous. I think that's sweet."

He smiled back at her. "Okay, what's up? You're being too cutesy."

"The truth is he has a 'thing' for Belle. She told him how delicious my cobbler was and he wants to make her one. He thinks that will give him an 'in' with her."

"That's wonderful!!"

"I thought you'd be pleased. I just hope Belle still brings treats for the kids."

"Well, maybe she'll be with Homer the next time." He put his arm around her shoulders and guided her to the dessert table. "Now can I have a piece of your chocolate cake?"

She leaned against him as they walked. "For you? I think if you're a good boy, you could have two pieces."

He kissed her on the forehead and looked deep into her eyes. "Is it as sweet as you?"

She pulled away and pointed to where he had kissed her and shook her head, whispering, "The kids."

"The kids are outside playing. Don't worry. I'm

keeping our truce when the kids are around."

"You'd better."

He put his finger to his cheek pondering. "Uh, did I promise to keep the truce when the kids weren't around?"

"You're a naughty boy. But to answer your earlier question, no, I'm sweeter than cake." She jokingly fluttered her eyelashes at him.

"We'll see about that. I haven't had the cake yet."

"You're right. You *are* impossible."

"Told ya so." He winked at her. "Growing on you yet?"

She let her breath out in a huff. "What am I going to do with you?"

"Want some suggestions?" he asked playfully while scooping up a big portion of the chocolate delight.

She could only shake her head at him. "Eat your cake, big boy. I'm going to find the kids." She grabbed up a plate of cookies and hurried out the door.

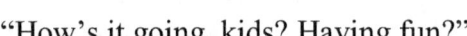

"How's it going, kids? Having fun?"

Beth was sitting on a bench beside a huge tree. She was cradling a sleeping Faye on her lap. "Not much."

"Well, I brought you all some cookies."

"No thanks," Beth said, staring off into space.

Cass knew better than to question Beth when she was in her mood, so she turned to the twins who were tossing a ball back and forth. "Want a cookie, boys?"

They both ran to her along with Mary who was jumping as high as she could trying to catch the ball as they threw it in the air. The three grabbed up their cookies and ran back to playing.

She turned to Dillon who was holding Bobby's hand and leaning against the tree near Beth. She offered the plate to him. He took one and gave it to Bobby, then meekly said, "Thanks."

Cass cleared her throat, wondering what was going on with Beth and Dillon. "Nice party, isn't it?"

Dillon shrugged his shoulders and stared at his feet.

Beth gave a rather stern look at Cass. "I guess if you call 'nice' watching you and Dad mooning all over each other."

Dillon raised his head and leaned toward Beth whispering loudly, "I told you not to say anything about that."

Beth pouted and said, "Well, it's true. You saw it."

Their argument brought Ronnie and Donnie to a standstill. "What's 'mooning'?" One of them said, both running over to Beth and Dillon with Mary following right behind.

"Wha- wha," Mary started, then sang, "Moooooning, whaaat is iiiiit?"

Cass stepped into the fray. "Kids, that's enough. There was no 'mooning'. Your Dad explained that we were trying to convince some people we were more than friends. That's all."

One of the twins came up to her, repeating, "What's mooning?"

"It's nothing to be concerned about, Ronnie."

"I'm Donnie."

She noted the tiny mole on top of his ear. "No, you're not. You're Ronnie."

"How'd you know?"

She smiled down at him and patted him on his head. "I know things."

Their giggling woke Faye and she reached for Cass. "Cass Mama."

Cass picked her up and kissed her on the cheek. "Just Cass," she said pointing at herself. "Say, Cass."

Faye pointed to Cass's face. "Cass Mama."

Cass let her breath out noisily, then looked at the others. "What would you all like to do? Play ball? Take a walk? What?"

Beth stood up. "We wanted to go swimming but we didn't bring our bathing suits."

Cass grinned. "Have you ever swam in your underwear?" She glanced around at all of their smiling faces at the prospect of going swimming.

Dillon shook his head. "Dad won't ever let us go to in the water without a grownup with us."

"I believe I'm classified as a grownup. Let's go. Is the water cool?"

"Actually cold," Beth told her.

"Sounds heavenly, but I don't think it's appropriate for me to strip down to my underwear like you kids can, so I'll just supervise."

Dillon started unbuttoning his shirt. "I actually have on one of Dad's undershirts that is so long I stuffed the tail into my boxers. It would probably come down past your knees if you want to cover your underwear with it and get in the water."

She thought for a long moment, then, "Sounds like a plan. Is there a private place I can change?"

"Lots of bushes," Dillon told her.

"Should I go tell your Dad where we're going?"

"No, he'll find us," Beth said. "We don't need him to come. The two of you together are..." She didn't finish her sentence when Dillon gave her a dirty look.

"Last one in is a rotten egg," Donnie called as he jerked off his clothes down to his boxers. He raced Ronnie, who had already shed his clothes. They jumped in at the same time and squealed when the cold water hit their bodies.

"Wait for the rest of us, boys," Cass said. "Remember, I'm supposed to be watching out for you."

Beth stepped out of her dress and plunged in. Mary followed suit. Cass pulled Bobby's trousers off him and let him wade in the shallow side while she held Faye and splashed the child's bare feet at the edge.

After a few moments, she counted heads and discovered one was missing. She turned around and saw Dillon still sitting on a stump in his boxers watching the others at play.

"Jump in," she called. "You're not sugar. You won't melt."

"No thanks. I'll just watch out for the others."

Ronnie ran out of the water, shivering and dripping water all over his big brother. "Dillon's a sissy. Dillon's a sissy," he sang.

"Ronnie! That is uncalled for." Cass glanced at Dillon who was plainly embarrassed. "Don't you know how to swim?"

Dillon shook his head.

"Beth, come take the baby and watch Bobby for me. I'm going to teach Dillon to swim."

Dillon's eyes grew big and round. "I...I don't...I don't think I want to. I almost drowned once and it scared me so bad. I can't."

"Of course you can. Everyone needs to know how to swim."

He reluctantly followed her lead into the water. When they reached a point where he could barely touch the bottom, she told him to bring his feet up while she held her hand on his back to keep him from sinking.

"Now relax. Lean back in the water until it covers the back of your head."

He stiffened.

"Whoops! Relax. If you don't relax, you'll go under."

He relaxed.

"Now, see? Just lie there like you're in bed. Keep your feet up, but don't force them up. Just let your body hang loose." She kept talking to him in a slow, calm manner until the boy's body hung suspended on its own in the water. She knew he was not even aware when she took her hand away.

"You're floating, Dillon," she said then caught

him as he tried to get up.

"I was?" he answered proudly.

"Now, we'll see if you can float on your stomach. Hold your nose and put your face in the water."

Dillon barely touched the water, then jerked his head back up.

"I'm not going to let you sink," Cass told him. "Just do the same. Relax like you did on your back only with your face in the water. Hold your nose and try again."

He did everything she told him and soon he was floating on his own.

Cass pulled him up. "See?" She kissed him on the cheek. "A few more lessons and you'll be a swimming champion. Now let's get out of here and eat the rest of the cookies before we freeze.

As they all sat on the bank eating their treats, one of the twins said, "Thanks, Cass. This was fun."

Manners? She smiled to herself. "Why, thank you, Ronnie. That was nice of you to say."

"I'm Donnie."

Cass turned toward the boy and noted the mole. "You are not. You're Ronnie."

Both boys giggled until they fell backwards. "How do you know?" they both asked.

"I told you. I have my ways," she answered mystically.

Bobby munched away on his cookie while laughing with his brothers. Cass pulled the little boy down next to her. "Can you tell who is Ronnie and who is Donnie?"

Bobby grinned really big and shook his head no.

"Obviously, you don't care," Cass said teasingly. "You have nothing much to say to either one."

This brought on another round of giggles from the twins.

Ronnie blurted, "You're kind of like a mom."

Before Cass could answer, Beth blurted, "She is not our mom and she's not going to be our mom."

The twins hung their heads low. Mary sat wide-eyed and studied Cass and Beth.

Cass felt a pang of pity for Beth. "Sweetheart, I'm not trying to take your mother's place. I couldn't, but can't we just be friends while I'm here?"

"Why? You'll just leave, like she did." She pointed over her shoulder up the hill. "She's buried up there in the Pine Valley cemetery."

Beth stood and looked up the hill where Beth pointed and saw several headstones. "I'm so sorry."

"Beth's voice softened. "I used to come here all the time, but don't so much anymore."

Cass walked over to a clump of wild flowers and carefully pulled them out of the ground. "Let's go there now."

Forgetting they were in their underwear, they all walked solemnly up to the gravesite and placed the flowers near the stone. The younger children ran and played, not knowing the seriousness of the occasion, but Beth and Dillon stood quietly and stared at the site.

Cass heard a heartbreaking sob and saw it was Beth. She put her arm around the young girl's shoulders and was sorrowful when she felt Beth tense at her touch. "You will always be in your mother's heart."

"I…I'm not afraid of her forgetting me," Beth explained. Tears streamed down her cheeks. "I'm afraid of forgetting her."

Cass clasped the locket that hung around her neck and thought of her own mother. "You don't have a picture of her?"

Beth shook her head, wiped her eyes with the back of her hands and scooped Faye into her arms. They all turned to start back to the river to get their clothes.

Just then Jake approached them. He peered off in the distance and twirled his hat on his finger.

What was making him so uneasy, Cass wondered? "Something wrong, Jake? Did the party not end well?"

"It went well…actually still going. I just wondered where you all were." His hat spun faster.

He still wouldn't meet her gaze. She took the time to admire how his blond hair shone in the sunlight. "Then what?" she prodded.

"Cass…you're…"

Suddenly it seemed they were all alone on the hill. Strange feelings overtook her. He was so handsome when he fidgeted like this.

He cleared his throat. "It's just an unlikely spot to find eight half-naked people running around."

Realization struck her. She glanced down at herself. Her heart pounded and she felt her cheeks aflame. Oh, my word! Blatantly standing in front of Jake Carpenter at his dead wife's grave wearing his damp undershirt.

Dried off, dressed and on their way home huddled in Jake's van, it seemed no number of apologies made up for the embarrassment Cass felt. "I am so sorry, Jake. I hope you don't think I was being disrespectful. It just happened so suddenly when Beth told me her mother was buried on the hill. We didn't even think about being undressed."

"No, I don't think that, Cass. I just didn't expect to see any of you up there. It's been a while."

She was relieved when Dillon changed the subject. "Dad, Cass taught me how to float."

Jake glanced out the corner of his eye. "I'll be darned. You got over your fear?"

"As long as she was standing by me so I wouldn't sink. It was awesome."

"He did really well," Cass added. "In fact, I think we all had a wonderful time at the river. Sorry if we worried you."

Beth piped up. "She wanted to tell you where we were, but I didn't want you to come. You two were enough to watch at the party. I didn't want…"

Dillon put his hand over her mouth.

Jake frowned. "Let her finish. What's upsetting you about Cass and me together at the party?"

Ronnie blurted out, "Mooning. Whatever that is."

Jake glanced at Cass. "We were 'mooning'?"

"I told you our little game wouldn't work out. It's confusing to the kids."

He looked in the rear-view mirror at the children. "Well, the Preacher Sunday party is over, so you kids can just forget about watching Cass and me 'moon'." He then turned to Cass. "Where do they come up with this stuff?" He winked at her. "I don't think I even remember how to 'moon' over someone."

She smiled teasingly. "Well, for someone with memory loss, you sure did a good job of it, Mr. Carpenter." She pointed to her forehead where he had kissed her at the party.

"See," Beth said, "they're doing it again. They're looking at each other with those 'moony' eyes."

Jake shook his head. "I think I need to monitor what Beth watches on TV a little closer."

Donnie yelled, "Ronnie, look at me!" He opened his eyes as big as he could and spread a silly grin across his face. "I'm 'mooning' you."

Ronnie stuck his tongue out and gave him the raspberries. "You look like you're 'gooning' me."

Cass burst out laughing.

Jake cast her an eye. "Don't laugh. You're only encouraging them."

"I can't help it," she said trying to stifle her hilarity. "They're a hoot at times."

CHAPTER SEVEN

After a light snack that evening, Jake put the kids to bed and Cass retired to the cabin. It had been quite a day for all.

While sitting in an easy chair pondering over the day's activities, Cass was still amazed how much she was enjoying her stay in Texas even though she knew she needed to move on and get her career as a teacher started. The school year would be starting in about a month, but still she had not had so much fun and hilarity with kids in her life...and Jake. What could she say about Jake? She knew she could always consider him a good friend just as he was to Sheila and Brad. Somehow it seemed more than friendship. She shook her head to put some sense back into her brain. Such a foolish thought!!

Just as she was about to crawl in bed, there was a knock on the door and she heard, "It's Jake. Are you asleep?"

"No, come in," she said meeting him at the door. "Are you okay?"

"Yes, I just want to talk...away from the kids. They're asleep. I feel I owe you an explanation about Lilly."

She shook her head. "No, you don't. It's really none of my business."

"I don't want you leaving here not knowing the facts." His eyes scanned her face for a few seconds, then added, "Maybe you'll understand Beth's feelings a little more."

"Beth is in my prayers. It's so hard to lose your mother...but I feel so bad for her if she hates God for her mother dying."

"That came about because so many parishioners said Lilly's demise was 'God's Will'. Beth took it wrong."

"Maybe if you know the whole story, you'll see why Beth is like she is."

"There is one thing that has puzzled me. Beth nearly always says her Mother left and talks about my leaving like her Mother did. You talk about Lilly dying, but Beth usually says her Mother left."

"I'll explain. Hear me out."

Cass nodded and motioned for him to sit in the chair while she sat on the edge of the bed.

Jake scanned her troubled features for a long moment, then let his breath out slowly. Settling back against the chair, he began. "You may as well know...everyone else does. It wasn't the first time Lilly ran away, just the last. This time she ran off with a man we learned was supplying her with drugs."

"I am so very sorry, Jake."

"Lilly wasn't a happy person. She suffered horrible bouts of depression and would just take off. Someone would usually let me know they saw her somewhere in another town, and I'd go bring her back. She was always okay for a while and insisted on having another baby." He frowned. "I tried to tell her it wasn't wise, but she would insist it would make her feel happy, but most times when she left it was right after having a baby." His voice broke into a sob.

Cass's heart felt it was breaking for this family. "Jake, you don't have to go on."

"I have to. I want you to know I loved my wife and wanted to do anything to make her happy, so she got pregnant." His eyes darted toward Cass. "You need to know I would not take a trillion dollars for my kids. It's just that I didn't want Lilly to do what she did after the pregnancy was over."

"There has never been a thought in my mind that you do not worship your kids."

His gaze lifted to the ceiling. "She never took to child rearing...except for Beth. She just wanted to bring them into the world. I really think she was trying to capture the joy she felt when she was pregnant with Beth. We were both overjoyed at the prospect of becoming parents. She stayed around after Beth was born but with the others, she was in and out."

"Did she want to go back to her family in California?"

Jake let out an ironic snort. "Her family disowned her when she married me. I was beneath her station, they said. Told her she'd be stuck in nowhere land stranded with a bunch of babies. I think that stuck in the back of her mind, although at first she was very happy here."

Cass nodded. "I can relate to what her family told her. My father said basically the same thing about my leaving the company to vacation in Texas. I don't feel welcome back home, although I will have to go back to Boston to see about teaching. It's the only place I know."

"I'm sorry."

"Don't be. It was my choice. Frankly, this is just what I needed. I feel alive again."

He smiled broadly. "That's good to hear. I thought maybe it was a little overwhelming for you."

She laughed. "It was at first, but I learned to relax and go with the flow." She turned serious. "But we got off the subject. What actually happened to Lilly? How did she die? Was it the drugs?"

"Not entirely."

Cass felt he harbored some ill-deserved blame for Lilly's death, and she wanted him to know she felt he did all possible. "I know in my heart you were a good husband."

He glanced at her. "Was I? I got her pregnant knowing she would leave soon after the baby or babies were born."

Cass never felt so much sympathy for someone as she did Jake. "You didn't know that for sure and she didn't either. She thought it would make her happy again. Isn't that what you said?"

"Yes, but it didn't work. She would leave, I

would find her, bring her back and it would be, 'let's have another baby' again." He hung his head. "After Faye was born, Lilly withdrew inside herself. No one could get through to her except obviously the drug dealer she met on one of her outings. Word has it he was about to be arrested when he decided to leave town and take Lilly with him. He was overheard telling her he would come for her while I was away at a cattle sale in another town."

"Oh, Jake!"

"The bad thing was she left the kids here alone. Good thing Beth was mature for her age. She had been bottle feeding Faye anyway since Lilly would not let the baby suckle."

"When did Lilly come back?"

"She didn't...not on her own volition anyway."

Cass's brows knitted. "I don't understand. She's buried..." Her hand started to point upward.

"Like I said, I was at a cattle sale when someone from town got word to me that she had left with him. By the time I caught up with the two of them, it was too late." He squeezed the bridge of his nose between his fingers. "They were in such a hurry to get away, the stupid idiot never slowed down for Deadman's Curve. I found them just outside of town. This time, I was too late to bring her back." He pulled a handkerchief from his pocket and wiped his eyes. "The car had overturned and rolled down the steep embankment. The doc said they'd probably been dead for several hours. I prayed she didn't suffer too long." He sobbed.

Cass rose and walked to him and placed her hand on his. "I don't know what to say."

He gently kissed the back of her hand. "There's nothing to say."

"Don't talk anymore. It's too upsetting to you."

"I'm okay. It's just that I haven't thought about that day for a long time." He shook his head. "When I got down to their bodies, I saw the car was riddled with pill bottles. They turned out to be strong drugs of all kinds. Lilly obviously thought she couldn't live without them." He drew a deep breath.

Compassion overtook Cass and she put her arms around his neck and held on tight. "I had no idea," she whispered. "The younger kids seldom mention her. Now I know why Beth asked me 'if someone did something bad would they would go to heaven'."

"Beth is probably the only one who actually understands the circumstances, but I'll never speak ill of their mother. She was loved by all of us."

"I'm sure."

"Probably there are those who think because we had so many children, we must have loved each other beyond reason. Well, it was like that in the beginning. She was everything to me…" His voice trailed reminiscently. "Then after a few years…there was something between us, but it wasn't love. More like hope. Hope to regain the feelings we once had for each other."

Cass pulled away from him and stood up, trying to hold back her tears.

He rose to stand beside her and took her hands in his. "I don't want to embarrass you, but sometimes a man and woman produce children even if there isn't much love between them. For lack of a better word, I'd say it's lust. I don't ever want that again. If I can't have pure love, I would rather not have a wife."

Cass dropped her hands from his. "I know about lust, Jake," she said shyly.

"You do?"

His questioning tone cut through her thoughts. "Oh, not that I...I mean..."

He smiled and put his hand on her shoulder to turn her facing him. "I never supposed you knew about it first-hand."

She lifted her head and her cheek brushed his fingers that rested on her shoulder. Warmth spread through her, and she felt uncommonly comfortable.

Their gazes locked, their smiles faded, and without realizing what was happening, he pulled her close and bowed his head. Hesitatingly, he lightly pressed his lips to hers.

An explosion of tender sensations chased her senses.

He lifted his mouth from hers and gazed into her eyes for a brief moment before capturing her lips again. This time he pulled her completely into his embrace. Her body felt galvanized to his. She had never had such a feeling.

Before she finished enjoying the taste and feel of him, he pushed away and was halfway through his apology before her mind came back to earth. "I know I said before that this would never happen again...and this will *not* happen again. I should never have..."

She put her fingertips to his lips, the lips she just tasted. "Shhhh. Don't say another word." She didn't want him to spoil the spell he had cast over her. She didn't have to be told nothing could become of this. She only wanted to enjoy the feeling of rapture a moment longer.

Early the next morning Jake felt he had been dragged through a knot hole. He laid awake half the night thinking about kissing Cass and the other half dreaming about it. The kiss was something he would never allow to happen again, but it was also something he knew he would never forget.

The children had to be the first and foremost consideration. No way would he subject them to another woman he 'lusted' for. Lust? No, it wasn't lust. Not with Cass. He respected her more than that. He didn't exactly know what it was with her. Desire for sure. After all, he's a man and she's a very desirable woman.

Riled from arguing with himself, he jerked on his clothes and ran to the barn. He heatedly shoveled feed into Dude's stall. "You don't know how lucky you are," he said to his horse. "You just have to pull a wagon or plow once in a while and wait to be fed."

He closed Dude's gate and trudged back to the house, mumbling to himself. "Heaven knows I wish I were a horse. Just plow a field and eat."

Cass saw him walking toward the house so she waited for him on the porch. "You're up early," she called to him.

"Couldn't sleep," he returned.

"Me neither."

"Kid's up?"

"Not yet. I was just about to start breakfast. Hungry?" she asked, trying to sound cheery although aware of what was bothering both of them. She turned and entered the house ahead of him.

Buck barked a welcome as Jake stepped up on the porch. Cass watched through the screen door as he gave the dog a scratch behind its ear. Her cheeks heated as she thought about facing him after last night's kiss. She quickly turned her back and pretended to be busy with breakfast.

Jake entered the kitchen and took a seat at the table. "Kids sleeping in today?"

Without turning around, she answered, "I thought I'd let them sleep a little longer. Rest up from yesterday."

"That's good. I've already gotten some of their chores done."

"That will make them happy, I'm sure."

Finally, she forced herself to look at him. Her heart danced in her chest and her hand trembled causing the cup and saucer to clank together. "Coffee?"

"Thanks." He took the steaming beverage, his brows knitted with concern. "Cass, about last night..."

"Forgotten," she blurted out and hoped God wouldn't strike her dead for lying. "You were feeling great sorrow. I was feeling compassionate." She waved her hand dismissing the discussion. "It just happened."

"Just got caught up in the 'game' we were

playing, huh?"

"Guess so." She gave a trembling smile toward his direction.

He sat staring for a long moment. "Cass, I want you to know I think a lot of you and never want you to think I expect anything from you other than friendship."

"I feel the same about you, Jake, but someone will come along one day that knocks your socks off."

"I think she already has."

"Jake…," she sighed. "We both know it could never go any further. To be honest, my heart goes out to the children for having an absentee mother, but I could never fill that void. They need someone with mothering instincts to give them a safe, nurturing home life. I've never been around children. I never even babysat during my teens." She thought of Beth's hostility toward her. "Also, they need someone who could elicit love and trust from all of them."

He stood up, drained his coffee cup and put it on the table. "I blame myself for letting this get out of hand. I know better than to start something I can't possibly finish." He started to walk out.

When she caught up with him and took hold of his arm, he jerked away. "Jake, don't blame yourself. It was both of us and I'm so very sorry."

"So am I," he said sadly and walked out the door.

Not another word was spoken about the night of the kiss for the rest of the week. Life went on pleasantly, and she and Jake exchanged small talk but the closeness they had shared was no longer present. Even the children noticed the change and were uncommonly well behaved and accommodating to anything asked of them. Even Beth asked Cass to help her with another dress for church, which Cass gratefully accomplished in time for church the next morning.

Cass looked forward to Jake's preaching and had practiced with the kids on their song so they could be the "stars" for the special music portion of the day.

Morning came and Cass hurried to the house to get a quick breakfast for all and help the kids get ready for church.

Having dressed Baby Faye in a sweet pinafore, she styled the child's hair in a fat curl on top of her head and tied it in place with a pink ribbon. She held a hand mirror in front of Faye. "Who's this?"

Faye grinned and kissed her image. "Pree Bebe."

"Yes, indeed. Pretty baby."

Faye touched Cass's cheek. "Pree Cass Mama."

Those words nearly brought tears to Cass's eyes. The last thing she wanted to do was let the kids get too attached to her. She knew she had overstayed her time here and needed to leave, but to where?

Mary and Bobby walked up to her with comb and brush, breaking into her thoughts. "Okay, kids, let's make you pretty," she said, then turned to Bobby, "and handsome."

As she brushed and combed their hair in place,

she noticed Dillon and Jake enter the living room. Dillon stuffed his shirttail into his trousers and then admired himself in the mirror that hung over the settee. He stood on a footstool to get full view.

"Look at me, Dad. All I need is a tie and I'd look all grown up like you."

Jake gave him a sideward glance. "You got a way to go," he said curtly.

Dillon gave his father a bewildered look. "You mad at something?"

Cass glanced up from tying Mary's hair ribbon and saw Jake's expression soften.

"No, son. Sorry I sounded harsh. I guess I got up on the wrong side of the bed."

Dillon went into a fit of giggles. "What bed? You fell asleep on the couch last night and were still there this morning."

Jake walked toward his bedroom. "I was working on my sermon and I guess time got away from me. I'll get my suit coat and we'll be ready to go."

Cass smiled at Dillon ribbing his father. "Sweetie," she said to the boy, "I have a dark blue scarf in my suitcase that I think could be perfect for a tie. Would you like for me to go get it?"

Dillon's grin was all the answer she needed.

She felt a tug on her skirt. Bobby looked up at her with sad blue eyes. She tweaked his nose. "I also have a small red scarf you can wear."

Bobby sprang into the one-legged jumping dance he always did when he was happy.

Cass started out the door toward the cabin. She called back to the twins. "Ronnie, do you and your twin brother need a necktie, too?"

"I'm Donnie."

"Don't try to kid."

She laughed when she heard him exclaim, "How does she always know that?"

Jake was waiting on the porch when she returned.

"I'll just be a minute," she said and entered the house.

She crooked her finger at the boys, signaling them to come to her. After tying the red scarf around Bobby's collar, he looked so cute in his man's shirt, she couldn't resist planting a kiss on his rosy cheek.

She tied the other scarves on Dillon and the twins and stood back to admire them. "So handsome, if I do say so myself." They looked in the mirror and smiled broadly.

Cass picked up Faye and they all went out on the porch to join Jake who was talking to Buck. "You watch the fort while we are gone to church, Buck."

It amazed Cass how Buck seemed to know what Jake said to him. She looked around. "Where's Beth?"

"I'm coming," came Beth's voice from inside.

When she emerged, Jake's eyes rounded in amazement. "Beth, you look so beautiful."

Beth smiled and pointed to Cass. "She did it…again."

Jake gave Cass a nod indicating his approval, but no words.

Cass was extremely inspired by Jake's sermon. He preached on love and it touched her heart in ways it had never been touched before. He mentioned that if you have faith, love will find you and you'll know the greatest joy God could ever grace you with.

It was the children's turn to sing their song, but they didn't want to do it without Cass standing up with them, so she took her place next to Jake with the kids next to her. Beth handed Faye to Cass and the rest held hands with each other.

The organist rendered the first chord and "Jesus Loves Me" rang loud and clear throughout the church.

Halfway through the song a stout middle-aged woman jumped into the aisle and yelled above the singing, "Lord, have mercy on my soul!" Her arms flailed momentarily, then she collapsed to the floor and moaned something about Satan clinging to her.

Cass glanced around. Jake and the rest of the congregation took no notice to the odd behavior. The kids went on singing, never missing a note. Cass kept her eye on the lady on the floor.

The woman let out a painful wail and Cass's hand went to her cheek. "Oh, my," she whispered. The lady rolled back and forth and kicked one leg in rapid succession like a cat with tar paper on its foot. With each kick, her stocking inched its way down to her ankle and her brown wig slid off her head to reveal gray hair.

Cass nudged Jake. "Pssst. I believe that lady's having a seizure. Shouldn't someone see to her?"

Jake bowed his head toward Cass and whispered, "That's just Verla Mae Henshaw. Don't worry about it." He straightened and continued to enjoy the children singing.

Cass poked him again with her elbow. "She's in pain."

Jake leaned down again. "She's kicking the devil out of herself."

Cass stiffened. "Kicking the devil..."

"Shhh. She can be a little sensitive about it. Especially when she loses her wig in the process."

Cass shut her gaping mouth but kept a close eye on Verla Mae Henshaw.

Jake patted Cass's shoulder. "It's okay. Verla Mae does this once a month or so. She'll come around in a minute, sock that brown hair back on and never know anything happened...except, of course, that the devil's gone for another month."

With a hesitant shrug, Cass resumed singing with the kids, but couldn't help glancing at Verla Mae from time to time. Just as Jake told her, after the kicking slowed to a twitch, Verla Mae sat upright, pulled up her stocking and placed the wig back on her head. Appearing no worse for wear, Miss Henshaw took her seat in time to join in on the last few words of the song.

"The Bible tells me sooooo," she sang out proudly.

Cass held her hand over her mouth to stifle her giggles. Verla Mae's wig was slightly askew and the gray strand sticking out from under looked like a long-tailed mouse running for cover under a fuzzy blanket.

As they stood outside the church, Jake introduced Cass to those who had not met her. They seemed to be very interested in Jake's "bride" to be. Cass's throat went dry as she looked at Beth who was staring an 'I-told-you-so' at her.

Clearing her throat in an attempt to change the subject, Cass smiled brightly and commented, "Didn't the children do great. Their music just warms your heart, doesn't it?"

Most parishioners nodded agreement, but some told Jake how proud he must be to find such a kind woman taking interest in his children.

When the last person passed through the line, Cass breathed a sigh of relief and turned to Jake. "I feel this has really gotten out of hand — this game we're playing."

"I'll admit, word has gotten around pretty quickly. It'll all work out."

"Yeah," Ronnie said, "it'll all work out. That is, if you marry my dad."

Cass felt so bad for the boy. She put her hand on his cheek. "Ronnie, you know that won't be happening."

"I'm Donnie."

She just smiled and shook her head no. "You know you boys can't fool me anymore."

Donnie spoke up. "She knows the difference because I'm the handsome one."

They all laughed, except for Ronnie who gave his brother a dirty look.

That night with all the children in bed, Cass said her goodnight to Jake on the porch and started to step down when Jake took her hand and pulled her back to him. She could feel the warmth of his body against hers.

"Jake, I need to go."

"In a minute. You've been so quiet since church; I want to make sure you're okay."

She breathed in slowly. "As okay as possible, I guess." She saw sympathy clearly in his expression. "It's just hard trying to fool others about us and not let the kids think the same. Living a lie is just not my cup of tea."

"Mine either, but I'll make sure the kids know it's just a temporary game."

She pulled away from his hold, but immediately wanted him to enfold her again. Dismissing the foolish feeling, she said, "By the way, you are a wonderful preacher. Your take on 'love' was so enlightening. Especially, the part about loving yourself and it will manifest itself into others."

"That's how I live. I have to have faith in myself and hope my kids learn to have faith in themselves."

"I know and I think it's working. When they sang their song, I could tell they were proud." She chuckled. "Even through Verla Mae's episode. That was really something else."

"The kids are used to Verla Mae. In fact, they said they want her to kick that 'old mean devil' out of this world."

"Wouldn't it be great if she could?"

He smiled teasingly. "Stranger things have happened."

She couldn't help but laugh and wave goodnight. "So I've heard...about a million times since I've been here."

CHAPTER EIGHT

———— ∽ ————

Cass helped Beth alter another dress and marveled at the idea of Beth wanting to dress up for church these days and even sit with the rest of the family.

Sunday was suddenly here and they were on their way to church again. Today another man was guest preacher. Jake said to 'brace' themselves when Pastor Freedman got cranked up."

The twins giggled. "Cranked is putting it mildly. He comes here a couple times a year but you can never forget him," Donnie said.

As they entered the sanctuary, the organist played several hymns while the congregation took their seats. There was a lot of friendly banter exchanged while the members greeted each other. Cass overheard comments about how nice the Carpenter children looked. She had to agree. The girls were so pretty and the boys so handsome.

When she glanced around, many eyes were on her. She smiled politely and noticed there was hardly an empty seat left. She was glad they arrived early enough to all sit together.

A teenaged young boy asked Beth if he could sit beside her. Cass smiled at Beth's blush when she said, "I guess so," then moved over slightly to make room. Cass started to change seats when Beth took her hand and said, "Sit here with me." Cass nodded and gladly stayed put.

Baby Faye had fallen asleep across Dillon's lap. Mary sat prim and proper next to Jake, smoothing her dress and touching the ribbon Cass had tied in her hair. Bobby squirmed between the twins, and Jake gave him a light thump on the back of his head. The boy quieted just before the preacher took his place at the podium.

Cass was surprised to see how young Pastor Freedman was. She'd pictured an older gentleman from the way the kids talked about him.

Her eyes widened when he raised his voice to a fevered pitch and banged his fist on the podium, telling them all to repent for their wicked ways. She thought of the 'game' she and Jake were playing and glanced at him, wondering if that was their 'wicked ways'. She saw that Jake was obviously thinking the same thing because he was eyeing her in the same way.

She was wrong to think the pastor couldn't get any louder. He certainly had a boisterous way about him, but she had a feeling that if everyone followed his dictates, they would land smack dab in the middle of heaven…without a doubt…smack dab in the middle.

Still breathless from the sermon, she barely had strength to sing the rollicking hymn the parishioners burst into when the pastor ended his speech.

As they rose to leave, the teenaged boy turned to Beth and said, "You sure look pretty today."

Beth's face turned red. "Thanks." She then took Cass's hand and said, "Gotta go." She practically pulled Cass out the church.

"I think he liked you, Beth."

"I know, but I don't like boys."

She looked up at Cass and smiled that teasing smile just like her father did on occasion. "What?" Cass asked.

"He looked like he was 'mooning' over me."

Cass broke into hilarity and hugged Beth to her. "You are wise beyond your years, young lady."

Looking up she was delighted when she saw a familiar face approach them. "Belle, so nice to see you again."

Belle gave Cass a hug. "You little thing you. I was telling Jake how beautiful Beth and Mary looked and he tells me you helped alter their dresses. Let me tell you, I could use your talent on some dresses if you ever find the time. SEW and SEW is booked up making wedding dresses and doesn't have the time for mine. Which reminds me, you'd better get your name in the pot if you want her to make your wedding dress. Have you set a date yet?"

Jake came to the rescue. "No, we haven't figured that out yet."

"Let me know when the big day is, but in the

meantime," she turned to Cass, "if you have the time, I could bring my dresses out…"

"I'm really busy, Belle."

"Oh, I'd pay you, of course."

"I would never take your money." She saw Belle's pouting lips. "Okay, I'll let you know if I have some extra time."

Just then Homer walked up beside Belle and locked arms with her.

Jake looked at her then Homer. "So, you two…?"

Cass smiled at Homer. "I guess the blackberry cobbler went over well."

Belle let out a loud hoot. "Homer will never win a cooking contest. Can't fault a man for trying though."

Homer hung his head and mumbled, "Should have written down the instructions. I think I left out some of the sugar."

Belle patted him on the back and then turned to Cass. "I've got the dishes you sent home with me. Sorry I never got back out there."

"No problem," Cass told her.

Belle smiled broadly and ran her fingertip down Jake's cheek. "You look mighty handsome today. "Course you always do." She stepped back and gave him a once over. "What's different about you?" She let out a boisterous laugh and poked him in the belly. "You filled out some." She leaned really close. "All that blackberry cobbler. Listen, sugar, you been enjoying too much of your fiancée's good cooking?" Adding, "Along with other good things?"

"Belle, I swear..." That was as far as Jake's words got.

Belle winked at Cass. "See how that preacher man kept looking at you?"

Cass's face flushed. "Probably just curious of who I am...like everyone else, I suppose."

"Or looking for a wife. He's single, you know."

Cass's cheeks became even warmer. "Belle, such talk!"

Belle pressed close to Jake again. "Better be setting that wedding date soon, sugar. You'll be losin' her to someone else if you don't watch out."

Jake smiled down at Belle. Cass froze in place. It was the smile she'd grown so fond of. The smile that had made its way into her heart, her dreams, her very soul.

She turned to see the preacher approach her. He extended his hand. "Miss Palmer, I presume."

"Yes, Pastor, so nice to meet you. I want to compliment you on your sermon. It did my soul good to hear such an inspirational message." She turned her eyes toward Jake who was still talking to Belle.

"I want you to know that when the time comes, if you haven't decided on who performs the ceremony, I'd be glad to oblige. Just get in touch with me and I'll come running." He smiled broadly.

Cass smiled back. "Thank you for your kind offer," she said, but thought, will this farce ever end?

Fortunately, Jake suddenly appeared beside her. "Ready to go home?"

"Definitely," she sighed.

As they walked away to gather up the kids, the preacher called out, "Remember my offer."

A solemn look came over Jake's face. "What offer is that?" he said curtly.

Cass had to laugh at his demeanor. "Not what you or Belle would be thinking. He offered to perform our wedding ceremony."

Jake let his breath out noisily. "Oh, that."

"Yes, 'that'. I hate to repeat myself, but this is getting out of hand. It's going to get harder and harder for you to explain when I leave that there was never going to be a wedding. I sure don't want to be in your shoes when they all know we lied."

"Hmmm, I'll cross that bridge when I come to it. In the meantime, I had a heart to heart talk with Belle. She won't be taunting us again about the wedding, or men looking for a wife, or my eating too much or anything."

"You didn't hurt her feelings, did you? I like Belle."

"No, of course not. I was tactful about it. She understands. Of course, she still wants you to sew for her."

"Come on, let's get the kids and go home."

That evening, Cass was sitting on the porch admiring the night sky when Beth came out and sat down beside her.

"Hi, sweetie. I thought you would be in bed by now."

"I wanted to talk to you. Dad's reading the Bible

and doesn't know I'm still up, so I'm going to talk soft."

"Okay." Cass was puzzled. "What do you want to talk about?"

"Did you hate God when your Mom died?"

"Oh, honey, of course not. It is not God's fault people die. Our faith in Him just helps us get through the sad times. We all have choices. We can wake up in the morning and choose to be sad or happy. I choose to be happy. My faith in God keeps me on the right path. I won't say I don't fail at times, but when you have faith it seems troubles pass more quickly. When I am tempted at something I don't know which path to take or what decision to make, I think, what would Jesus do. In fact, I have a bracelet with those words on it. My mother gave it to me when I was young."

"How do you get faith?"

"Prayer. I pray every night and thank God for all the good things I have in life and all the good things to come. I know you have gone through some of the saddest times a young person should ever have to go through, but believe me time is a good healer. In time, with God's help, you will be happy again."

Beth twisted the tie on her robe. "Sometimes I'm kind of happy now. I feel like I shouldn't be."

Cass put her arm around the girl. "Oh, sweetheart, don't feel guilty about being happy with your life. You are one of the most caring people I have ever met. The way you take care of your siblings, and never complain about it. It is very commendable. That is a trait I also admire about your dad. Sheila and Brad told me he was the nicest man they knew and I'll have to agree with them. It has rubbed off on all of you kids."

Beth smiled. "Except the twins."

Cass laughed. "Even the twins. They mean well. They are just full of energy and like to get a rise out of us."

Beth rose, then turned back. "Cass, thanks for everything you've done for us. Dad explained you are trying to do the right thing, but I'll be honest with you." She hesitated before continuing. "I think he's in love with you."

"Oh, no, honey. Strong like maybe, just as I have a strong like toward him."

"Whatever." After a second, she said, "I'm going to try to get faith. I don't want to hate God anymore. It makes me too sad."

Cass stood. "Come here." Beth did so and let Cass embrace her tightly. "Love you, Beth. You're the sweetest."

Beth looked up at her with tears in her eyes. "I know you love us kids. I also know you don't want to hurt my dad, but you will when you leave." She turned and walked into the house.

Beth's words haunted her through the night. She didn't want to hurt anyone.

Her cell phone ringing brought her out of her melancholy mood and she was shocked when she saw who was calling.

"Hello, Father."

"Cass, so good to hear your voice."

"Are you okay? I'm surprised to hear from you."

"I'm better than okay. Here's something you probably never thought you'd hear from me. I'm sorry. Sorry for the way I treated you when you left."

"Father, I don't know what to say."

"First, call me Dad. Father is not personal enough for me anymore."

"What's happened to you...Dad?"

"Well, I hired a lady to take your place at the company and she's working out very well. In fact, I have become very close to her. Her name is Glenda. She's close to my age and, I don't know how it happened, but we bonded almost immediately. I invited her to dinner one evening, and she said she would come if I went to church with her first. Well, since I wanted to get to know her better, I went to church knowing I'd be bored to death."

"And?"

"And, you were right. Something came over me...a kind of relief and well-being. I've been praying and it feels good to know God is there when we need him. Again, I'm so sorry it's taken me so long."

"Don't apologize. I'm just very glad you believe. That makes me so happy. I would love to meet this Glenda...and, Dad, I'm happy you found someone who makes you happy."

"You make me happy, too, sweetie. I want you to come back home. Get a job teaching or whatever you want to do, just come home. I love you."

"Oh, Dad, I love you too and miss you."

"Then you'll come home soon?"

"I've been thinking about coming back to Boston to teach."

"By the way, you won't have to worry about running into Kyle ever again. That bright idea he had that he wanted you to invest in was starting his own company exactly like Palmer Corporation. Actually, Glenda clued me in on what he was doing when she had a conversation with one of our clients he was trying to get to switch to his company. I guess he thought if you invested in it, the confidentiality agreement he signed when he joined our company would be null and void. Threatened with a lawsuit or leave Boston, he opted to leave and never come back."

"Yea for Glenda."

"Okay, then I'll see you soon. Love you a bunch."

"You, too, Dad."

As she disconnected a feeling of joy came over her. Her father, now Dad, was able to show love. She had not seen that in him since her mother died years ago. Being welcomed back home should make her feel elated. That's what she wanted, wasn't it? Then why did she feel so hesitant about it.

She walked toward the house. Buck met her with a rousing bark and lick on the hand.

"Hi, friend," she said to him. "Wish you could talk. I need someone to give me some good advice." The dog licked her hand again. "I know. You'll miss me. I'll miss you too."

Jake called from the front porch, "Buck, leave the lady alone!"

"It's okay. I've gotten used to his amorous

ways." She smiled and gave Buck a scratch behind his ear.

When she walked up the steps, Jake handed her a cup of coffee. "Thanks." She took a sip, then sat down. "My Dad just called."

"Really? How did that go?"

"Actually, better than I could ever have imagined. He has met a woman who invited him to church and it has rubbed off on him. He said he was sorry and wants me to come back home. He has even been praying." She shook her head. "I never thought I'd see the day."

Jake took her hand. "That's wonderful, Cass. I know that has weighed on your mind for a long time. I'm happy for him...and you." He stared off in the opposite direction. "Does that mean you'll be leaving right away?"

"If I want a teaching career, I'll need to. The school year starts in a couple weeks and I'll need to get my application in." Tears sprang to her eyes. Why am I crying? She rubbed her eyes with the back of her hand.

"You'll certainly be missed," Jake said sadly.

"So will you...be missed, that is. I'll miss the kids, Buck, all of this." She waved her hand around.

"Well, just let me know when you are ready to go and I'll drive you to Houston. No sense in you taking the shuttle from Pine Valley."

"Oh, Jake, you don't need to go all that way."

"I want to. It would give me more time with you."

Tears again ran down her cheeks. "Jake, please don't make this harder than it is. I'm leaving because I only want the best for you and the kids."

"And you don't think you are…the best for us?"

She felt her heart breaking. "I don't know what I am right now. I'm going back to the cabin. I need to think."

"Don't you want breakfast? I'll get out the breakfast food."

"Thanks, but I'm not hungry."

She left quickly and returned to the cabin where she fell face down on the bed and cried her eyes out for the next hour. Then she got up and pulled her suitcase out from under the bed and started packing her belongings. She came across her jewelry case and saw the 'What Would Jesus Do?' bracelet and decided to give it to Beth.

The door opened and in came Buck followed by all the kids.

"Hi," she said sadly.

"Dad said we needed to come say goodbye. He said you'd probably be leaving today," Beth told her.

"I think it's better. If I stay any longer…"

"You won't want to go?" Ronnie asked.

Cass smiled at his sweet face. "Something like that."

"Then the thing to do is stay a little longer," the other twin said. "Do you know which one of us is speaking?"

"I know who you are, Donnie." She smiled and patted him on the head.

The three-year-old tugged at Cass's hand. "I'm Bobby."

All turned to the little boy with mouths agape.

Cass took him in her arms and rocked back and forth. "You spoke. I'm so proud of you. What else can you say?"

"Don't go."

That broke her heart. "I have to, sweetie."

Baby Faye looked at her with teary eyes. "Cass Mama, no go bye, bye."

"How can I explain to a baby." Cass kissed her on the cheek.

Mary came to her and put her arm around her waist. "Who will sing with us after you're gone?" She spoke without a sign of a stutter.

"Oh, honey, you sing so well by yourself. Just keep doing what you do?"

"Who will sew my dresses?" Beth asked.

"Kids, I'll miss all of you, but you'll get along just fine." She set Bobby down on the bed and turned to Dillon whose head was bowed low. "You know how much I think of you, Dillon. You are the perfect example of a gentleman. I couldn't be prouder of you if you were my own child."

"I'd love to be your son," he said so low she barely heard him.

She had no words to say to him. It was all just too sad.

Buck whined and licked Cass's hand.

Dillon patted the dog on the head. "See, Buck wants you to stay, too."

Beth approached Cass and looked up at her. "I hope I didn't make you want to leave because I was rude to you. I'm sorry for that."

"Oh, honey, you don't have to be sorry. I knew where you were coming from. You'd lost your mother, you'd taken on grown-up duties and were very protective of your siblings...and your father, too, for that matter. I understood. You are not the cause of my leaving."

Cass retrieved the bracelet from her jewelry box. "Here, Beth, this is for you."

Beth took it and smiled broadly. "Thank you so much." She put it on her wrist and whispered, "What Would Jesus Do?" She reached in her pocket and pulled out the gift she wanted to give to Cass. "This is for you."

Cass studied it for a moment. "Sweetie, this is the jewelry you made for your Mother."

"I know. She didn't want it. Ronnie said you were like a mom. I want you to have it."

That did it. Cass broke into sobbing tears and couldn't stop for several minutes. She was wiping her eyes when Jake walked in.

"Kids, I said to give your goodbyes, not upset the lady."

"They didn't," Cass said. "They have been very sweet." She looked around at all of them. "Did you know Bobby spoke?"

"Wow!" He looked straight at Cass. "You certainly do wonders. I can't count the wonderful things the kids do since you came. You must have magical powers."

"She does," Ronnie interjected. "She always knows who I am and who Donnie is."

Jake laughed. "That is definitely magical." He turned to Cass. "Are you sure you want to leave all this hilarity?"

Bobby came forth. "No."

Jake was amazed. "Look at that." He picked the boy up and kissed his cheek. "Tell her to stay."

Bobby blurted, "Stay!"

"You all are making this so hard." Cass wanted to hug the breath out of all of them...even Jake. Jake. Suddenly it dawned on her. She was in love. She had never known the real feeling of love until she met Jake. She thought it was just liking him, but Beth was right. It was more than like. It was love, and she couldn't imagine her life without him in it.

Beth turned to her dad. "Tell her. Tell her how you really feel about her before it's too late."

He looked down at his daughter. "How do you know how I feel about her?"

"We all know."

"Yeah," Donnie said. "You look at her with 'moony' eyes."

That made them all laugh, especially when Jake opened his eyes wide and stared at Cass. "Like this?"

Cass laughed harder. "If you had looked at me like that, I think I'd have run for the hills."

His laugh dwindled to a smile. "Beth's right. I need to tell you how I feel." He took a deep breath. "I am in love with you, Cass. Deeply in love, and I want you for my wife. I know in my heart you are good for the kids. If I didn't think that, I would never have said a word."

All the kids yelled, "Yes!!!!"

The heaviness in Cass's heart lifted and brought her sheer joy. "Oh Jake, I love you, too. I think I knew that for a while but didn't know the real meaning of love until now."

Jake pulled her into his arms and kissed her passionately. When he pulled away, he asked, "Then, will you marry me?"

"Yes, yes, yes," she answered just before he captured her lips again.

Bobby jumped around on one leg as the other children clapped hands and smiled while Buck howled and turned circles around everyone.

Cass stepped away, picked up her cell phone and called her dad.

"Dad, I won't be coming home, but I'd like you and Glenda to come here."

"Why's that?" he asked.

"I put you on the speaker so all could hear. I'm in love with Jake Carpenter and he has asked me to marry him. I need you here to give me away."

"Well, this is a surprise, but I think we could manage that. When?"

"We haven't set the date yet."

"Hello, Mr. Palmer. Jake Carpenter here. I want you to know I love your daughter very much and will do everything in my power to make her happy."

"I love her more than life myself, and I know you'll be good to her. I talked to Brad the other day and he told me Cass was in good hands at your place. Made me feel better about her being in Texas. I got the feeling a wedding wouldn't be all that surprising to him."

Jake smiled at Cass and mouthed, "Told you so."

She nodded and went on with her conversation. "Dad, I also wanted to ask if you are ready to be a grandpa?"

"You're pregnant?"

"Heavens no. Be a Grandpa to Jake's seven kids."

"Well... what did you say? Seven?"

She smiled at Jake. "That's right. Seven of the most amazing children you'll ever meet."

"You did say seven."

"Seven," she repeated.

All the kids yelled, "Hi, Grandpa-to-be!"

"After you meet them, you'll fall in love...just like I did."

"I'll take your word for it. Sounds like quite a group. Just let me know when we should be there."

"I will, Dad. Love you."

"Love you more," he said before disconnecting.

She turned to Jake. "Now all we need to do is set the date."

"How about tomorrow?"

She laughed. "I think I need a little more time than that. Like Belle said, I need to go to SEW and SEW and put my name in the pot for a wedding dress."

Dillon spoke up. "Tell her to put a rush on it."

Jake nodded agreement. "We need to call Sheila and Brad and tell them if this was their plan all along, it worked, so they better get ready to be maid of honor and best man."

"I agree."

Jake pointed to her suitcase and said, "Go ahead and pack up. I think we need to move you to the house now. You can have my bedroom and I'll sleep on the couch until we tie the knot...which I hope will be sooner than soon.

Bobby said, "Sooner, sooner, sooner."

Jake laughed. "If Bobby's going to repeat everything, we'd better watch what we say."

Cass kissed each child one by one, then turned to Jake and kissed him over and over on his lips, on his cheeks, on his neck, then back to his lips for a long, long moment.

"Who would have thought I'd go on vacation and fall crazy in love with a Texas farm, eight people and a dog."

"Oh, stranger things have happened," Jake said teasingly.

"Name one," Cass returned.

"I'll get back to you on that. I'm busy right now...kissing you."

He cradled her face in his hands and gently planted a mind-boggling kiss on her eager lips. When the kiss ended, she laid her head on his chest and wrapped her arms around his waist as he hugged her tight. This was as close to heaven on earth as she could ever imagine.

Yes, a vacation in Texas was indeed just what she had needed.

ABOUT THE AUTHOR

Norma resides in Branson, Missouri, where she and her husband, Gary, sing gospel music in and around the Springfield/Branson area. She hopes her faith in God is reflected through her music and her writing, because faith is her greatest source of inspiration for her songs and her stories.

OTHER PUBLICATIONS

A woman's Touch
Heavens to Betsy
One Special Christmas

Children Did You Know, Easter Bunny Believes
(Children's book)